CRITICAL ACCLAIM FOR
BARRY GIFFORD AND
ARISE AND WALK

Please turn the page for more extraordinary acclaim. . . .

BOOKS BY BARRY GIFFORD

FICTION

Arise and Walk
Night People

The | Wild at Heart
Sailor & Lula | 59° & Raining (Perdita Durango)
Novels | Sailor's Holiday
Sultans of Africa
Consuelo's Kiss
Bad Day for the Leopard Man

New Mysteries of Paris
A Good Man to Know
Port Tropique
Landscape with Traveler
An Unfortunate Woman
Francis Goes to the Seashore
A Boy's Novel

NONFICTION

The Devil Thumbs a Ride & Other Unforgettable Films
A Day at the Races: The Education of a Racetracker
The Neighborhood of Baseball
Saroyan: A Biography (*with Lawrence Lee*)
Jack's Book: An Oral Biography of
Jack Kerouac (*with Lawrence Lee*)

POETRY

Ghosts No Horse Can Carry: Collected Poems 1967–1987
Giotto's Circle
Beautiful Phantoms: Selected Poems
Persimmons: Poems for Paintings
Poems from Snail Hut
Horse hauling timber out of Hokkaido forest
The Boy You Have Always Loved
Coyote Tantras
The Blood of the Parade
Selected Poems of Francis Jammes
(*translations, with Bettina Dickie*)

ARISE

AND

WALK

ARISE
AND
WALK

a novel by

BARRY GIFFORD

A Delta Book
Published by
Dell Publishing
a division of
Bantam Doubleday Dell Publishing Group, Inc.
1540 Broadway
New York, New York 10036

ISBN: 0-385-31472-8

Reprinted by arrangement with Hyperion

Manufactured in the United States of America

Published simultaneously in Canada

July 1995

10 9 8 7 6 5 4 3 2 1

BVG

FOR VINNIE DESERIO

and to Sparky
from Buddy

And Jesus knowing their thoughts said,
Wherefore think ye evil in your hearts?
For whether is easier, to say, *Thy* sins
be forgiven thee; or to say, Arise, and walk?
—Matthew 9:4–5

Despair is the only unforgivable sin, and it's always reaching for us.

—Sam Peckinpah

ARISE

Arise, and WALK

SALVATION
READ
ROMANS
10:9 & 10

SALVATION
READ
ROMANS
10:9 & 10

Top Snake

THE REVEREND CLEON TONE, formerly pastor of the Church of the Fresh Start in Daytime, Arkansas, stood on the corner of Burgundy and Orleans streets in the French Quarter of the city of New Orleans, holding upside down in his hands a battered black felt fedora. Suspended from his neck by a piece of string was a hand-lettered cardboard sign that read, HAND YURSEF A FRESH START BY LEND A MAN A HAND. "The Lord'll love you harder," he said whenever a passerby dropped a coin into his hat.

Cleon Tone, who now slept in a nameless hotel patronized chiefly by transients on North Rampart Street, was fifty-eight years old. Thin strands of gray hair spiderwebbed his skull; his facial skin was splotchy, pink and red; his hands were dotted by liver spots. Black smudges scarred his throat, indelible souvenirs of his attempted murder by Prentiss Temoign, the husband of Viridiana Legend Temoign, a member of the Church of the Fresh Start, whom Tone had cuckolded a decade before. Owing to that disgraceful incident, the reverend had fallen on hard times, having been railroaded out of Daytime, Arkansas, by his irate former parishioners. He had drifted around the Deep South since then, initially working at odd jobs until his worsening alcoholism reduced him to this present state.

The night before, Cleon Tone had shut himself inside the W.C. and while seated on the toilet had picked up off the floor a section of the previous day's *Times-Picayune*. He read an article about the mating habits of pit vipers, such as rattlesnakes and copperheads. Female copperheads, he learned, mate only once every three to five years. When one emerges from her den after hibernating for the winter, she is greeted by a veritable phalanx of suitors. These males battle one another for the privilege of partaking of her favors not by biting but by wrestling, attempting to force the other down to the ground into a submissive position, an exercise that may last hours or even days, about the same length of time it takes to complete the process of copperhead copulation. Females shun the weaker snakes, and even younger males will assert themselves over the defeated adults, whose self-confidence has been severely reduced. Once the competition has been completed, Cleon Tone read, the top snake seeks out the willing female and immediately presents her with his double-pronged demand.

"Be damn!" Cleon said aloud, after he had finished with the article. "That been me, the top snake! Now look."

The knob rattled and the W.C. door shook.

"You-all about crapped out, yet?" someone asked.

"Clinch it back a minute!" Cleon said.

He tore the page he had been reading in two and used a piece to wipe himself. The other he folded up for another time. Reverend Tone pulled up his trousers, fastened them, and pulled the flush chain before sliding back the bolt and opening the door. To his surprise, the hallway was empty when he emerged.

"A top snake don't lay down for long," he mumbled, as he shuffled toward his room. "And this'n got at least one big strike left in him, you bet."

WET HEAT

WILBUR "DAMFINO" NOUGAT and Gaspar DeBlieux slumped down in their red leather easy chairs in their two-bedroom suite at the DeSalvo Hotel on Gravier Street, drinking rum and orange juice, waiting for the two hookers they had ordered from the Congo Square Escort Service to arrive. Nougat and DeBlieux—pronounced "W"—were white men in their mid-forties, in New Orleans for the annual national convention of dental supply salesmen, the profession at which each of them had been laboring for the better part of twenty years. Nougat lived in Nashville, Tennessee; DeBlieux in Monroe, Louisiana. They had become friends fifteen years before, when they had first shared a room at the Pontchartrain in Detroit. Since then, they had arranged to stay together whenever and wherever the dental supply salesmen of America gathered.

"More an' more I'm likin' dark meat," said Gaspar. "Used to it was only blondies stood Little Boy at attention. Why I married Dolly Fay, 'cause of her yellow hair, which now can't no way tell for sure what color it is. Changes every month or two. 'Bout you, Wilbur? What's your preference?"

"Damfino or care, Dublya. Long's it's hooters a pair an' wet heat below, she can be blue with white polka dots from hair to there. Stick it and lick it, that's the ticket."

DeBlieux laughed. "Sonesta hear what you say, she'd be after you with her magnum cocked."

"Only cock she get, too," said Damfino. "Woman size the Goodyear blimp now. You ain't seen her in a year or two. Awful how she let herself go."

"Sorry to hear it. Sonesta was sweet-lookin' once."

"She claims it was havin' a fourth child did in her figure, but it's chocolate. Sonesta can't go a hour without she's chunkin' chocolate."

There was a knock on the door.

"Be our dates, Dub."

Damfino popped up, went to the door, and opened it. Two tall, lanky black hookers entered the room and stood together, unsmiling, in front of a large picture window opposite Gaspar DeBlieux.

"Drinks, ladies?" asked Damfino.

The hookers had tough faces; their heavily painted skin looked waxed. Both of them were quite beautiful, however; each had high cheekbones, full lips, and what appeared to be a perfectly sculpted figure barely contained by a tight leopard-skin dress. They wore red berets over their pressed black hair.

"Holy Infant!" chirped Gaspar, springing out of his chair. "Looks like we hit the right number tonight!"

He practically pranced around the hirelings, grinning, the contents of his hand-held glass sloshing onto the burgundy carpet.

"We don't use alcohol," said the slightly shorter of the two prostitutes. Her voice was very deep.

"If you don't mind," said the other, in a more feminine tone, "we'd prefer dispensing with the business side up front. Two hundred each, gentlemen."

Wilbur Nougat and Gaspar DeBlieux each extracted two crisp C-notes from his wallet and handed them over. The prostitutes took the money and deposited it in their purses, out of which they each then withdrew a .32-caliber Smith and Wesson revolver with a silencer affixed to the barrel. They pointed the guns at the men, who froze at the sight.

"Take off your clothes," said the tallest hooker.

"Just a hot damn minute," said DeBlieux. "What you doin'?"

"Take off your clothes or we'll shoot you," said the other hooker. "We be aim low."

The men removed their clothes and stood naked in the middle of the room.

"Suck his dick," the shorter hooker commanded DeBlieux. "Genuflect front your partner an' do 'im."

"This the buddy system," said the taller one.

Gaspar dropped to his knees, put his lips on the head of Damfino's penis, and closed his eyes.

"Suck it off!" the taller one repeated.

Gaspar DeBlieux did his best, but Nougat's penis remained flaccid. Tears rolled freely from both men's eyes.

"Maybe you do it better," said the tallest tormentor. "Trade places. We ain't goin' till the faucet starts flowin'."

The men did as they were told and this time Nougat got some results. Gaspar's penis hardened despite his fear.

"Stroke it," said one of the hookers, Damfino didn't know which, and after a few minutes he made DeBlieux come.

"Swallow it!" ordered the taller hooker.

Damfino dropped his head to the floor and sobbed. Gaspar stood, trembling, his depleted penis shrinking rapidly.

"Y'all get down again," the smaller hooker said to DeBlieux, who obeyed.

Both men bent forward, their eyes shut tight. The hookers lifted their short dresses with their free hands, took out their penises, and urinated on Nougat and DeBlieux.

"Surprise!" the prostitutes shouted, mirthful now, giggling like schoolgirls.

When they had finished, the hookers straightened their skirts, replaced the guns in their bags, and walked out of the room, leaving the men wet and shivering on the hotel room floor.

Outside the DeSalvo, Cleon Tone stood about ten feet from the entrance, wearing his HAND YURSEF A FRESH START BY LEND A MAN A HAND sign and holding his hat. As the regal, leopard-skin-clad hookers walked by, the taller of the two dropped a hundred-dollar bill into the disgraced pastor's fedora. Before the occurrence had registered on Cleon's brain, his benefactors had climbed into a taxi and sped away.

The Reverend Tone stared at the glowing C-note, shook his head, and said aloud, "The Good Lord got Him some sundry damn messengers, don't He?"

THE BRAVE
AND THE BEAUTIFUL

*C*LEON HAD A SOLID CUBAN DINNER of ropa vieja, frijoles
negros, arroz amarillo, plátanos maduros, flan, and café
con leche at the Country Flame on Iberville Street, then
decided to treat himself to a movie. It had been several years
since the Reverend Tone had seen a film. He strolled up Canal
to the Choctaw Theater and was horrified to find that the
asking price for entry was six dollars. This being a special
occasion, however, Cleon paid for a ticket to see *The Brave
and the Beautiful*, starring Martine Mustique.

Martine Mustique had been born Rima Dot Duguid, in Bay
St. Clement, North Carolina, a place she fled at an early age.
After two failed teenage marriages and a half-dozen abortions,
Rima Dot Duguid, who at twenty called herself Sarita Touché,
left Atlanta, Georgia, where she had lived for four years, for

France, in the company of an Iranian art dealer named Darwish Noof. In Cannes, she was spotted sunbathing topless on the beach by Tora Tora-Tora, the Tahitian synthetic cosmetics king, who hired her as a model for his company's new perfume, Paroxysme. It was Tora-Tora who renamed her Martine Mustique one paradisiacal afternoon on the veranda of his estate on the Caribbean island whose name she now wore as her own. The transition from magazine supermodel to film star was a swift one for the once–white trash Carolina runaway.

The celluloid flesh merchants had promoted Martine Mustique as another Rita Hayworth or Ava Gardner, advertising her as a throwback to more glamorous days. She had starred in one box office blockbuster after another, always in tandem with the worthiest leading man of the moment. Even the names of her films—*Forever Ruthless, Lost Among the Living, The Big Ache, Tame Me!, I Am Desolate*—were redolent of an earlier, seemingly purer era, however mistaken such a notion might be. Deluded or not, the adoring multitude attended Martine Mustique's movies as if on a religious pilgrimage.

When she was found murdered—decapitated—in the bathtub of her house in the Hollywood hills, the public outpouring of grief was titanic. Her killer, a spurned suitor named Edgard Veloso Shtup-Louche, the young scion of Shtup Industries, manufacturers of forty-five varieties of condoms, mailed a confession to the Los Angeles Police Department before hanging himself in a gazebo on the Shtup-Louche estate in Bel Air. In his letter, Edgard said that Martine had refused his proposal of marriage after forty-eight hours of virtually continuous lovemaking. She had been, claimed Shtup-Louche, the only woman with whom he was able to achieve an erection. When she denied him her hand, she denied him his only chance for lifelong happiness. Rather than murder all of the psychiatrists who had attended him since childhood, Edgard said—though that certainly should be done, he added—it was easier just to do away with the object of his affection, and, of course, himself.

The Brave and the Beautiful had been completed two days before Martine's death, one week prior to what would have been her thirtieth birthday. Since its release, this last evidence of her remarkable ability to charm even the most reluctant and cynical among moviegoers had broken box office records worldwide. In life, Martine Mustique had beguiled; in death, she transfixed. Cleon Tone was no less mesmerized as he watched her final portrayal, that of a Croatian lion tamer named the Great Vukovara, who is torn between her love for her home and family and a Serbian soldier during the Yugoslavian civil war.

Cleon wept with the others in the theater as the Great Vukovara learns that her lover has been killed by Croat freedom fighters just before she must stage a command performance for the queen of England. She goes on as scheduled, and for her finale, Vukovara tosses aside her whip and chair and orders the lions to attack her. As the big cats tear Vukovara apart, ripping and rending in a spectacular frenzy, superimposed on the screen is a picture of Martine Mustique at her most beautiful, the way she looked in her first ad for Paroxysme. The effect on Cleon Tone was devastating.

When he finally managed to extricate himself from his seat and stumble out of the theater, the disgraced reverend and other patrons were confronted on the street by a troop of skinheads dressed in leather jackets with their trouser legs tucked into the tops of their black boots, holding signs saying, DON'T BLAME KROTZ IF THE KOUNTRY ROTS and SAVE OUR TOTS, VOTE FOR KROTZ, along with poster photos of Klarence Kosciusko Krotz, the Real American Party (RAP) candidate for governor of Louisiana. Klarence Krotz, Cleon Tone knew, once had been the Great and All-Powerful Grand Beast of the Holy Order of Everlasting Yahoos (HOOEY), a white supremacist group headquartered in Tensas Parish, in northeastern Louisiana.

Later that night, lying on the cot in his room on North Rampart Street, it occurred to Tone that it would cleanse his soul for good if he were to eliminate from the planet a hater such as Klarence Kosciusko Krotz. By this consummate act, Cleon could come to terms with his own fall from grace, and redeem himself in the eyes of the Lord and those who had suffered from his own selfish behavior. He could then arise, and walk with the angels. The next day, Cleon Tone decided, he would purchase a tool of destruction. He then turned his attention to his own tool, masturbating with the image of Martine Mustique in his mind until he reached a state approaching paroxysm.

HISTORY IN
THE MAKING

DORTORINA RIDICULO KROTZ was the daughter of a department store bookkeeper from Alexandria, Louisiana, named Torquemada Ridiculo, an immigrant from Barcelona by way of the Azores, and Sallie Gay Crews, who had been born and raised in Alexandria. How Torque Ridiculo came to Louisiana, Dortorina, his and Sallie Gay's only child, never had known for sure. As well as she could ascertain, her father had landed initially in New York City and the company he found work with had then relocated to Alexandria, taking Torque along. Torque had died of the Pyongyang-B strain of influenza when Dortorina was six, so she had only her mother's version of the events of Torque's life to go by.

One time, when Dortorina was fourteen, after her mother had imbibed one too many Absolut and Orange Crush cocktails at a neighbor's backyard barbecue party, Sallie Gay said that Torque had been an illegal alien on the lam from some embezzlement scam up north when she married him. When Dortorina tried to talk to her mother about this the next day, Mrs. Ridiculo had dismissed the story entirely, saying she could not imagine having said such a thing.

Dortorina married Thaddeus Kosciusko Krotz, a traveling cement salesman from Grand Coteau, when she was eighteen and he was forty-four. Krotz's people were originally from Poland, but their part of the country had been annexed by Germany during the Second World War. Shortly after the annexation, Thaddeus had deserted from the Nazi army, into which he had been drafted, and made his way to America by stowing away on a general cargo boat sailing from Liverpool, England, to Baltimore, Maryland. That ship, the *Duke of Earls Court*, was torpedoed and sunk in the North Atlantic six weeks later.

While on board the *Duke of Earls Court*, Krotz stole one of the crew's seaman's papers along with some money, and he managed to fake his way past the Customs officer at the port of Baltimore. Thaddeus spoke virtually no English at this time, but he found work quickly at a variety of menial jobs; first around Baltimore, then as he moved south, fleeing the kind of cold weather he had detested in Poland.

Louisiana was his last stop. Acadia Parish, with its large Catholic population and warm climate, appealed to Thaddeus Krotz, and he hired on as a mixer at the Acadia Cement Works. Within a year, Krotz became a salesman for the company, and shortly after his marriage to Dortorina Ridiculo the former Nazi infantryman was allowed to purchase shares in the business. Fifteen years later, he became its majority stockholder; five years after that, he renamed the company Krotz Cement, and soon the Krotz name was known as the largest manufacturer of cement in the Deep South. Thaddeus diversified his interests, buying up radio stations and newspapers in small towns from Texas to Florida. By the time Dortorina's and his only child, Klarence, was confirmed, Krotz Industries was firmly entrenched in the lower echelon of the *Fortune* 500.

Thaddeus and Dortorina died together in a small-plane crash during a lightning storm while flying from Jackson, Mississippi, to Shreveport, when their son was twenty-three. Klarence, who had graduated the previous year from LSU and was at the time of his parents' deaths enrolled in law school at Duke, discontinued his studies and assumed the directorship of Krotz Industries.

It was not long before the idea of holding political office began to appeal to him. At twenty-six, Klarence ran for a U.S. congressional seat and, using the family-owned radio stations and newspapers to apprise voters of his attributes, won easily. After five consecutive terms, however, Krotz, by this time a conspicuous reactionary presence in Washington, D.C., decided to return to Louisiana and run for governor. If he could accomplish this feat, the next step, even amateur political observers surmised, would be back to Washington, toward the White House.

Klarence Krotz had never married but he was seen often in public in the company of lovely young women. Known around Washington as one of that city's most eligible bachelors, Krotz seldom dated the same woman more than once or twice, a fact that led so-called insiders on Capitol Hill to consider the dashing Louisianian as something of a playboy. This conjecture, however, could not have been further from the truth. These young women were merely a cover for Krotz's predilection for older, European pederasts, men who bore some resemblance to his father, Thaddeus.

Washington, D.C., of course, was a virtual playground for

18

Klarence, inhabited as it is by a fluctuating population of foreign diplomats. Had it not been for Zvatiff Thziz-Tczili, a sixty-eight-year-old lobbyist for the Bulgarian sardine industry, who had become Klarence's close companion during his most recent term in Congress and who was about to retire, Krotz probably would not have decided to run for governor of his home state. It was at Zvatiff's suggestion that Klarence now set his sights on Baton Rouge, encouraged by his companion and mentor in world diplomacy to look ahead, to use the governorship as a necessary stepping-stone to the presidency of the United States.

Thziz-Tczili had lived and worked in Washington for nearly forty years, and in Klarence Krotz he saw the first serious hope for a genuine new world order since the golden days of the Axis powers. Krotz was young, handsome, and prone to a type of intellectual infantilism Zvatiff Thziz-Tczili felt confident in his ability to manipulate. In Klarence, the Sofia-born sardine power broker believed he had found his Trilby, his ultimate tool. That it would have come in the form of an heir to a Louisiana cement manufacturing fortune Zvatiff could not have guessed, but he trusted his intuition. When Klarence knelt before the old Bulgarian and took into his mouth the mottled, thick, short but still powerful Eastern European organ, Thziz-Tczili felt the blood of human destiny course through his veins. He and Klarence Kosciusko Krotz, Zvatiff felt, were about to make history.

DAY OF THE MULE

CROESUS "SPIT" SPACKLE, thirty-two, a member of the Holy Order of Everlasting Yahoos, and Demetrious "Ice D" Youngblood, twenty-eight, a member of the El-Majik Nation, an African-American prison gang, hacksawed their way through the bars on a cell window in the De Soto Parish jail at Mansfield, Louisiana, then dropped down two knotted bedsheets to freedom. The white supremacist and the black separatist had escaped together after watching *The Defiant Ones*, a 1958 movie, on TV in the jail recreation area. In the film, Tony Curtis and Sidney Poitier star as southern convicts, one white, one black, who are on the run from the law while shackled together. Though they hate each other, the men in the movie are forced to live like Siamese twins, finally coming to respect and care for a person they had been bred to despise.

The Defiant Ones had inspired Spit and Ice D, who figured correctly that the guards would not consider the possibility of their assisting one another, having housed them together in the first place out of plain meanness, in the hope that the two men would do each other severe bodily harm. However, Ice D had fashioned a crude hacksaw out of a bedspring, and the supposed foes worked in concert until the hundred-year-old iron bars gave way. Each man was intelligent enough to recognize their having been exploited by the guards, and their bond as fellow rejects of the system was strong enough for them to decide to stick together once they were loose outside the walls.

"Spit," said Ice D, as they made their way toward Highway 49 through the woods just west of Ajax, "we the kind of men can make a difference we try, you know?"

"What you mean, D?"

"Mean I'm tired as you takin' table scraps."

"Hell, yes. I been beat like a rented mule, you can witness. Time the mule have his day."

"Ain't no black or white about it, neither, Spit. You dig? The man dump dirty water off the porch, he don't pay no mind who stand below."

"Tell you, D. Other day I heard on the news the Kluxers over in Gainesville, Georgia, wanted to enter a float in the local Christmas parade titled 'I'm Dreamin' of a White Christmas.' "

"Forgive me not laughin'."

"Didn't strike me funny, neither. City official found some excuse to cancel the parade. Didn't want to deal with that."

"You still support that HOOEY All-Powerful Beast motherfucker?"

"Klarence Kosciusko Krotz. Not no more, D. I ain't got no leader."

"I'm gon' kill the fool, Spit. Like you to help me."

"What about your boy, El-Majik? He ain't no different."

"Okay, Spit. We kill him next. First Krotz, then El-Majik. What you say?"

"Least we can do, D. We can't put some good in the world, might as well take out some bad."

~~The~~ $\mathcal{T}$HE $\mathcal{S}$ECRET
OF THE $\mathcal{U}$NIVERSE

*W*HEN HE WAS A BOY, Cleon Tone decided that he would be the one to discover the secret of the universe. His Southern Baptist parents took him to church regularly, he attended Sunday School, but Cleon did not entirely bite on the concept of creationism. At eight and a half years old, the future preacher inclined more to scientific reckoning than he did toward blind purchase of the idea of the Garden of Eden.

During a discussion of Adam and Eve one Sunday noon, the perspicacious Cleon announced to his class that it would be he who correctly ascertained the origin of man. His Bible studies teacher, an unmarried woman in her late thirties named Myrtis Wyatt, took a piece of bituminous coal the size of a hockey puck from the top drawer of her desk, pried apart the blaspheming boy's lips, and forced it between them.

"And the Lord said unto him," Myrtis Wyatt pronounced, her hands holding firm Cleon's birdlike shoulders, " 'Who hath made man's mouth? or who maketh the dumb, or deaf, or the seeing, or the blind? have not I the Lord? Now therefore go, and I will be with thy mouth, and teach thee what thou shalt say.' "

From that time forward, Cleon Tone never questioned the explanation for man's place in the universe or gave expression to his thoughts in regard to an alternative genesis. Myrtis Wyatt never did marry, and at the age of fifty-six, while pruning roses in her wheelchair-bound mother's garden, a mud wasp invaded the tympanic membrane of the spinster's right ear, where its sting proved fatal. Myrtis's paralyzed mother sat watching her daughter writhe in agony on the ground while the winged insect crawled deeper and deeper into the aural cavity. The old woman was entirely helpless in the face of death, a distinction that allowed her a momentary kinship with those persons more abled than she.

CLOSE CALLS

"*D*ID YOU KNOW that beginning on this day in the year 1916 the temperature at Browning, Montana, fell a hundred degrees in twenty-four hours, from forty-four degrees to minus fifty-six?"

"Don't say."

"Best believe it. Yesterday in 1932, a hundred-yard-wide tornado ripped through Gibson County, Tennessee. Killed ten members of a family of thirteen whose home was swept away."

Cleon was seated at the counter of Plain Annie's Eatery on Toulouse Street having a morning coffee and jelly doughnut. Coco Navajoa, a retired prizefighter in his late forties who once had been the number-five-ranked featherweight boxer in the world, according to *Ring* magazine, sat on Cleon's right, smoking a Pall Mall. Coco was a weather freak who lived on

St. Philip Street in a room filled with books and magazines and newspaper clippings having to do with meteorological events.

"What about tomorrow?" asked Cleon.

"In 1938, the great aurora over southeastern Europe was characterized by a fantastic brilliant red display and gave an illusion it might be the reflection of a gigantic fire below the horizon. Hundreds of fire engines raced toward the horizon from many parts of the continent. The same day in 1961, the worst ice storm in the history of the state of Georgia closed most of the schools and state roads. This condition lasted two days."

Two men, one black and one white, entered the eatery and sat down on counter stools to Cleon's left. Plain Annie, Cleon observed, served them black coffee. The two new customers wore shabby clothes and were in need of a shave.

"How about the day after tomorrow?"

Coco clucked his tongue and grinned. "A real red-letter day," he said. "Belouve, La Réunion Island, in the Indian Ocean east of Madagascar, set the world twelve-hour rainfall record of 52.76 inches."

"Coco, you oughta get some TV station to hire you," said Plain Annie, a compact, red-faced woman of indeterminate middle age whose thumb-high black roots betrayed her platinum mane. "Better a genuine weather scholar, such as yourself, rather than them failed actors they got can't hardly locate the prompter. More coffee, men?"

"No, thanks, Annie," said Coco.

"Just a drop," said Cleon.

"Couple mean-lookin' boys there," Annie whispered as she poured. "Fresh from Angola, you ask me."

The reverend-in-exile glanced their way, then raised the cup to his lips.

" 'And the mean man boweth down, and the great man humbleth himself,' so saith Isaiah," he said.

" 'Surely, he scorneth the scorners: but he giveth grace unto the lowly.' Proverbs," Coco added.

"Charity ain't never been my specialty, I admit," said Plain Annie, who then moved down the counter.

"Freshen that for ya?" she asked the two strangers.

"Sure," said Spit.

"Obliged," said Ice D.

"You fellas from close by?" Annie asked.

"Depends what you calls close," Ice D said.

"We just quit the air force," said Spit. "We was stationed at Keesler, over to Biloxi."

"Bet you-all're pleased not to be prisoners no more."

Ice D glared hard for a moment at Annie, then relaxed after Spit said, "Yes, ma'am. We just lookin' now to be prisoners of love."

" 'Love is strong as death,' sang Solomon," Plain Annie said, and almost smiled.

"Reckon them is strong-arm boogers," Coco confided to Tone.

" 'Be not forgetful to entertain strangers: for thereby some have entertained angels unawares.' Hebrews," said Cleon.

"In 1957, on a warm and sunny July afternoon in Wilmington, Delaware, a dust devil suddenly appeared and tore roofs off several houses."

"What's that supposed to mean?"

"Don't count on the weather," Coco said, "even when the sun's shinin'."

Going Down That Road Feeling Bad

"Oh, the law they never got him, 'cause the devil got him first," sang Ray Bob Realito as he unlocked and pushed aside the accordion security door in front of Rebel Ray Bob's Pawn & Loan on the corner of St. Claude and Elysian Fields avenues in New Orleans. He next turned off the burglar alarm and let himself in the main entrance, closing the door behind him. Ray Bob reversed the hanging sign behind the glass panel from CERRADO to ABIERTO and continued to hum his favorite tune. He turned on the overhead fluorescent lights and made his way to and behind the pawn counter, where he pushed the power and play buttons on the VCR set up beneath a small platform featuring a fifty-inch monitor that could be viewed from any part of the shop.

Two automobiles tore along a country road in glorious black

and white on the screen above Ray Bob Realito. One car was chasing the other at night. The cars were old, 1950 Ford sedans, and the face of the driver of the lead car remained hidden as he skillfully outraced and eluded his pursuer. Ray Bob busied himself at the counter and did not turn to look at the picture until the credits rolled.

Thunder Road, a 1958 movie about moonshiners starring Robert Mitchum, was Ray Bob Realito's all-time favorite film. He played the video every day in his pawnshop on the fifty-inch screen. He kept the sound off, since he knew every word of dialogue and each lick and lyric of the title song, which had been co-composed by the star, Robert Mitchum, who also had co-written the story on which the screenplay was based. Mitchum had recorded the title tune in 1958, and it had been a big hit at that time. Ray Bob never understood why someone else had sung it on the movie sound track.

It was Robert Mitchum, of course, who was driving the lead Ford in the opening sequence, sticking it to the federal agent, who was no match for the supreme runner of illegal alcohol in the South. In the movie, Mitchum outruns and defies both government agents and organized crime thugs looking to muscle him out of business; but neither they nor either of two women can claim him before Satan steals away with the legendary driver.

Ray Bob Realito was sixteen years old when he first saw *Thunder Road* at La Sal de la Vida Drive-in in Chicken Neck, Texas, where he had been born and raised, and the movie had deeply affected him. The strong, stoic Mitchum character, the man who never complained or made excuses for deals that derailed or went bad, was the kind of person Ray Bob aspired to be. He felt that Klarence Kosciusko Krotz, the Real American Party candidate for governor, was such an individual, and Ray Bob had tacked up a blue and white VOTE FOR KKK—

THE REAL AMERICAN WAY poster on the inside of the store above the front door so that customers could see it on their way out.

The Realito family had been dirt poor during Ray Bob's boyhood. His parents had worked as pickers in the cotton fields of East Texas, and so had he and his older sister, Victoria China. Ray Bob had left Chicken Neck, Texas, soon after seeing *Thunder Road* and joined the army in Houston. After his discharge, he worked in the oil fields around Morgan City, Louisiana, saved his wages, and bought into what was then called Rebel Billy's Pawn & Loan. The owner, Billy Shores, taught Ray Bob the business, and following Shores's death Ray Bob took over and changed the name to his own. Ray Bob had lost touch with his people soon after his enlistment. All he knew of them since that time was that they had left Texas and moved west, probably to California. His parents were illiterate, but Victoria China, who had attended school, as had Ray Bob, through fifth grade, wrote him once when he was at boot camp, saying she was going to have a baby and that she planned to kill it as soon as it was born.

Ray Bob sat down on a two-step swivel stool with a wicker back support and opened his copy of *Where the Money Was*, the autobiography of Willie Sutton, the famous bank robber. When a reporter asked Sutton why he'd robbed banks, Willie replied, "Because that's where the money is." Ray Bob believed in reading a book a week. Last week he had read *Rip Ford's Texas* by John Salmon Ford, a memoir by the nineteenth-century soldier and Indian fighter. Next week Ray Bob planned to delve into *Tales of the Angler's Eldorado,* Zane Grey's chronicle of his fishing exploits in New Zealand. Not only did reading help to make the time pass as he waited for customers, but Ray Bob believed the exercise to be a proper substitute for travel. These days Ray Bob never left New

Orleans, his feeling being that the psychological uncertainty occasioned by travel elevated the blood pressure and therefore constituted a life-shortening threat. Ray Bob's desire was to live well into the twenty-first century, long enough to witness order having been restored in the country. Then he would not have to go down that road feeling bad. Klarence Krotz, Ray Bob thought, might be the first unfaltering step in that direction.

The door opened and two men entered: Cleon Tone and Coco Navajoa. Ray Bob interrupted his perusal of Willie Sutton's description of a scene in One-arm Quigg's pool hall in 1921. Happy Gleason was giving Willie the bad eye and Ray Bob knew some serious shit was about to fly so he hated to stop reading, but there was a front door and it was unlocked between nine and nine, during which hours anyone might walk in, and sooner or later, Ray Bob knew, they did,

"Need me a piece," said the reverend. "Iron won't choke timin's crucial."

Ray Bob took a good look at Cleon Tone. Selling a man a weapon of terminal destruction was not merely mercantilism but a matter of conscience.

"What's your price range?"

"Twenty-five. Thirty most."

Ray Bob brought up a handgun from below and laid it down on the worn mahogany countertop.

"This here's a rare enough beast. H&R .32 five-shot. Field-tested nigger shark, kept oiled. Twenty-seven fifty, take it home and pet the daylights out of it. Stay-put-type piece."

Cleon picked up the gun and inspected it from every angle.

"What you think, Coco?" he asked the ex-boxer.

"Us Hispanics, man, we know knives, not guns."

Cleon took out two twenty-dollar bills, tossed them on the counter, and said, "Deal."

Ray Bob said, "Throw in a dozen cartridges and we'll call it thirty, how about? Just sign the arms register here and fill in an address."

Cleon nodded and picked up a pen that was next to an opened logbook and signed, "Rev. C. Tone, formerly Daytime Ark., now N.O."

Ray Bob put a box of bullets and a ten where the twenties had been. Cleon put the .32 in one pocket of his jacket, his change and the box in another.

"Take special care, gentlemen," Ray Bob said to the men's backs.

He opened his book and read, "Despite the fact that his left arm had been amputated, he would set the pool stick in the crook of his arm, just above the stub, and he could beat just about anybody in Brooklyn."

*P*RECIOUS

"*Z*VATIFF, come listen! She's on!"

Zvatiff Thziz-Tczili licked the sardine juice from his fingers and hurried from the kitchen to the den, where Klarence Krotz was watching television. Klarence had recently become addicted to the broadcasts of a televangelist prophetess named Presciencia Espanto, and had made Zvatiff, who had never seen or heard her, promise that he would watch the show with him tonight.

"Sit next to me," Klarence said, when Zvatiff came into the room. "She hasn't said anything yet."

Presciencia "Precious" Espanto was thirty-six years old. She had been born in a small village near Puerto Angel, Mexico, on the Gulf of Tehuantepec, where she lived until she was six, at which time her family moved north, crossing the border illegally just west of McAllen, Texas. In McAllen, her father, who was known in his native village as El Profeta, was killed in a bar fight by a fellow patron who took exception to his prediction that the president of the United States would die in Dallas during an upcoming visit to that city.

After the death of El Profeta, Presciencia and her younger twin sisters, Esplendida and Espiritosa, were taken by their mother, Despareja, to Houston, where Despareja worked as a prostitute. Presciencia left Houston when she was sixteen in the company of a traveling power tool salesman named Ed Ard, who paid Despareja five hundred dollars for the privilege. Presciencia traveled with Ed Ard around his territory, the Southwest, for four months, until she ran away in the middle of one night while he slept off a drunk in the Brazo Negro Motel in Gila Bend, Arizona. She never saw Ed Ard or her mother and sisters again.

Presciencia worked as a hotel maid in a number of towns and cities until she realized that, like her father, she had the gift of prophecy. In Las Cruces, New Mexico, Presciencia started her own ministry, which she called La Iglesia de los Ingratos—the Church of the Ungrateful—based on the assumption that human beings can never entirely appreciate the gift of life until it is taken from them, and must therefore remain ungrateful until their ascent to heaven or descent into hell. At first Presciencia's followers were mostly Mexicans, farm workers, ranch hands, and domestics, but as word spread about her ability to prophesy, a wide variety of people, including whites and Indians, joined her church.

Because she was an illegal alien, Presciencia moved often, communicating by letter and telephone with those who could not follow her. Eventually she was deported, but regained entry to the United States shortly thereafter by legal means at the behest of the wife of a U.S. senator from Louisiana who

34

had become a believer. It was because of Sally Blaine, whose husband, Senator Rantoul "Bingo" Blaine, was later killed in a plane crash over Big Tuna, Texas, that Presciencia came to establish the Church of the Ungrateful in Baton Rouge. After the Espanto teachings reached cable TV, Klarence Krotz, among tens of thousands of others, became fascinated by this female preacher, eager to hear her every word and witness her healings and prophecies.

The old Bulgarian pederast and his protégé sat transfixed before the electronic image of Presciencia Espanto, her long, curly blond hair contrasting dramatically with her burnt-sienna skin. She wore wraparound dark glasses at all times now, to protect her inner harmony from vision thieves, and covered her body with a plain white cotton robe. Only Sally Blaine, the former senator's widow, and now Presciencia's lover, knew that beneath it the prophetess was naked. Seated behind Precious on the stage were her bodyguards, several young Hispanic men recruited from the No Chingues gang in Albuquerque.

"Hear me, ungrateful ones," Presciencia said, her golden head bowed toward the microphone. "Hear the black wings as they beat above, above and beyond. Hear the words of Jeremiah: 'Behold, he shall come up as clouds, and his chariots shall be as a whirlwind: his horses are swifter than eagles. Woe unto us! for we are spoiled . . . wash thine heart from wickedness, that thou mayest be saved. How long shall thy vain thoughts lodge within thee?' Oh, thou ungrateful, what of your expectations? 'When thou art spoiled, what wilt thou do? Though thou clothest thyself with crimson, though thou deckest thee with ornaments of gold, though thou rentest thy face with painting, in vain shalt thou make thyself fair; thy lovers will despise thee, *they will seek thy life*. For I have heard a voice as of a woman in travail, and the anguish as of

35

her that bringest forth her first child, the voice of the daughter of Zion, that bewaileth herself, that spreadeth her hands, saying, Woe is me now! for my soul is wearied because of murderers.' "

"She's the one, Zvatiff, the one person we need to put us over the top," said Klarence, muting the sound of the television with his remote control.

"Her people, they will vote?"

"They'll vote if Precious tells them to vote. They'll do whatever she says. If we can get her to back me, it'll show the niggers and the nigger lovers that a prominent person of color believes in me. It'll turn 'em around without turnin' off the Kluxers, who'll figure rightly it's a political necessity. I don't have to explain myself to them, they know who I am and always will be. Forget the Jews; we'll take care of them after."

The sardine doyen nodded and danced the stubby, oily fingers of his right hand over his bald head.

"We shall meet with her, then," Thziz-Tczili said. "It would be good if she will prophesy your victory."

Klarence smiled and placed his right hand over the old man's crotch.

" 'Though they dig into hell,' as Amos says, 'thence shall mine hand take them; though they climb up to heaven, thence will I bring them down,' " said the candidate. "Miss Precious and I, between us we got the world by the balls."

$\mathcal{E}$LOHIM

S PIT AND ICE D needed new clothes.

"El-Majik always sayin', a brother in need come to one of his Welcome Homes," said D, "supposed they provide him food, clothes, shelter in return for do some work. Sell they paper, *Majik Speak,* or somethin'."

"That ain' hep me none," Spit said.

"I take extra for you, Spit. Don' nobody be knowin' the diff'rence."

The two escapees sat on a bench in a small, triangular park on Magazine Street, smoking cigarettes.

"You know where's this Welcome Home in New Orleans?" asked Spit.

"Looked it up in a phone book back at that café. Be on

Napoleon Avenue. Nearabouts, I think. Why don't you wait here an' I go see what up wit dem?"

Spit sat alone on the bench and thought about how messed up everything was. Here he was, a grown man, an escaped convict without a cent except what he could steal, in need of clothes and shelter, partnered up with a black, intent on assassinating two men for the crime of lying in public.

Being poor was a condition with which Spit was not unfamiliar. His single most horrifying childhood memory was of the time he had come into the house and found that his mama had fallen asleep in a chair while breast-feeding her newest born. The child had fallen asleep also and lay still in her lap while a gray-brown rat the size of Spit's daddy's shoe nibbled at the nipple of his mama's left breast. Spit, who was seven years old when this happened, had tried to knock the rat off his mama, but the rapacious rodent bit into the woman's breast, causing her to awaken with a shriek and drop the infant to the floor.

Spit would never forget the sight of his mama twirling and howling in pain as she attempted to dislodge the gigantic rat. Her horrifying dance seemed to go on interminably while Spit watched and his baby sister cried. Finally, the Spackle mother managed to tear the beast from her chest, flinging the thing across the room as she collapsed. Spit had seen the rat float through the air as if in slow motion and land on all fours with his mama's left nipple locked in its protruding teeth, then scurry away with the lactating treasure.

The breeze blew a piece of newspaper against Spit's right ankle and he reached down and picked it up. It was the front section of a week-old *Times-Picayune*, and Spit read a small item on the back page:

EMBASSY SOUGHT FOR EXTRATERRESTRIALS, was the heading. The story was taken from the Deutsche Presse-Agentur and datelined Geneva. "A sect that says it represents extra-terrestrial beings wants an embassy in Switzerland," Spit read. "Claude Vorhilon, head of the 250-member sect that claims to be in contact with extraterrestrial beings called 'Elohim,' wants to put the embassy question to a nationwide vote."

Spit crumpled the newspaper and tossed it aside.

"Be double damn if this planet ain't already loaded with surplus crazy bastards per square inch," he said aloud. "End's near they start lettin' in ones from outer space."

MOVING RIGHT ALONG

"**Y**OU ARE LOOKING WONDERFUL, Sally, as usual."

"Why, thank you, Zvatiff. I'm not entirely displeased to see that you are still alive, either."

Sally Blaine and Zvatiff Thziz-Tczili sat together at a table against the wall in Galatoire's. This was their first meeting since both had established residences in New Orleans, Zvatiff having only very recently taken an apartment in the Garden District from which to direct Klarence Krotz's campaign in the southern portion of the state. They had first met and become acquainted, of course, in Washington, D.C., but had not been in touch since the death of Rantoul "Bingo" Blaine. Following up on Klarence's interest in Presciencia Espanto, Zvatiff's investigation had disclosed her relationship with Sally

Blaine, and subsequently he had arranged a meeting with the widow of the deceased senator.

The former lobbyist for the Eastern European sardine industry ordered turtle soup, pork chops, and hearts of palm. The televangelist's mistress requested salad only.

"You are quite trim as it is," said Zvatiff. "Why not have something more?"

Sally laughed, and replied, "Remember what Jack Kerouac said: 'I'd rather be thin than famous.' "

"Who is this person who speaks such absurdities?"

"A novelist."

"Ach," said Thziz-Tczili, frowning as he raised his wineglass, "novels! I never read them."

As Zvatiff and Sally Blaine lunched and arranged a suitable time and place for Precious and Klarence to rendezvous, Cleon Tone stood in the Maria Callas Memorial Launderette on Conti Street reading a flyer tacked to the bulletin board next to a washing machine in which the backslidden reverend had deposited his clothes.

"El-Majik Speaks!" Cleon read. "Do Not Let This Happen To You! Where are the people who have disappeared? Every year countless people disappear without a trace never to be seen again and it is never reported. Why? I am convinced that they are the victims of Followers of Elohim, an evil, extraterrestrial anti-Human that is heavy into organized crime who practice ritual murder on a massive scale and sell the flesh to fast-food chains to make hamburgers out of and in this way dispose of the evidence.

"What these people do is entrap persons looking for sex, then kill them in a very sadistic manner and these things are generally done fairly close to the fast-food restaurant. Another method is that they buy children from poor whites whom abduct the children from school yards, daycare centers and even from their parents by pretending to be health care workers or from the child protection agency. Usually it is black children who are the victims. These people generally target single mothers who have problems to begin with or welfare recipients who no one would believe, and that I am convinced is the reason they have artificially created a high birth rate among welfare recipients. If we do not stop it, no one else will.

"Why do the criminals get all the breaks? Why does the law only protect the other guy? Why does every TV show concern crime? The answer is that the Elohim are running the media and using it to create an unusually high crime rate in order to have an excuse to take your freedom away. The Elohim are Outer Planetary parasites who hide themselves among us. They often profess to be either Jews or Christians but they are not. They manipulate political candidates such as KKK and espouse insane notions via false prophets.

"I am convinced that the media has a secret archive where the Elohim keep movies of an anti-Semitic and anti-Christian nature and blackmail the clergy of this nation and Rome for millions in order to keep them off the air.

"The Elohim used Saadam Hussein to kill Kurds and use the hides for leather and sell the flesh to fast-food chains to make hamburgers out of. Elohim like to ingest live human sperm and vomit caviar that hatches into maggots that eat mulberry leaves and spin cocoons and hatch into full-grown people who do the same.

"The Elohim have schools in Russia and Romania that train people to manipulate the human mind and send them over here to cause unstable people to commit acts of violence to use as an excuse to enslave the public. They are trying to create a junkie work force that they only have to pay in drugs. Where will it all end?

"Salemm' Aleikoum. Yours in peace everlasting, El-Majik."

"Dis yo wash?"

Cleon Tone turned and confronted a humpbacked old lady about four and a half feet tall with a black patch over her right eye. The front part of her scalp was completely bald and dotted with scabs.

"Ah look yoost, yaw done. Done stop, see?"

Cleon opened the lid and unloaded his few articles of clothing.

"All yours, ma'am," he said to the woman, who cackled.

"We dogs," she said, wagging her head. "Watch yo ass, mist, watch yo ass. God dog git it, haw!"

ßUGS

*I*T WAS NOT REBEL RAY BOB'S CUSTOM to return to his shop once he had closed it, but he had forgotten to take with him earlier in the evening a shortwave radio he intended to fool with. He was convinced that some of the languages he heard on it had to be coming in from outer space. There was no way, he figured, a human being on planet earth could work their mouth around some of those sounds. It was eleven minutes past midnight when Ray Bob unlocked, entered, and then closed the front door. Three seconds later, before he could turn on a light, a blunt object—a chunk of heavy glass with the word MIZZOU decaled on it in gold letters over a black and gold drawing of a snarling tiger—permanently wrinkled the unsuspecting owner's right temple, causing his immediate collapse onto the brown-stained cedar board floor.

"Wad you hid 'im wid?"

"Ashtray."

Ice D knelt next to the prone pawn king and closely inspected his head.

"He fix, Spit. Fix permanen'. Maybe bes' we carry 'im out back way we come in."

"No," said Spit Spackle, slipping the murder weapon into the canvas sack that already held the several guns and ammunition he and D had swiped from the store. "Bugs be on him too quick. Cop scientists use insects now to establish time of the crime."

"Insex? How you know dis?"

"Read it in a magazine in the prison library. Dead body lyin' outside attracts enough blowflies and flesh flies to lay thousands of eggs in the mouth, nose, and ears within ten minutes of death. The eggs hatch about twelve hours later into maggots that feed on tissues. When the maggots is done, they crawl off the body and cocoon in the soil around it. Then comes more bugs, beetles usually, that chow down on the dryin' out skin. After them it's spiders, mites, and millipedes that feast on the insects. Best we just leave him."

"Damn!"

Ice D stood up and the two fugitives took off out the front. Spit slammed the door behind them, dislodging from the wall next to it a framed sign that flipped faceup onto Rebel Ray Bob's back. It read: IF ASSHOLES COULD FLY, THIS PLACE WOULD BE AN AIRPORT.

THE RING OF TRUTH

"**W**HAT TIME do we meet these gentlemen?"

"Six. Suite at the Monteleone."

"Little higher, please, Sal. It's always where the wings was itches most."

Presciencia Espanto stretched her brown form to its full length. She lay flat on her stomach on the bed while Sally Blaine straddled the hottest female televangelist since Dilys Salt and massaged her back. Both women were entirely nude, having spent most of the afternoon making love and sleeping.

"It still rainin'?"

Sally glanced out the closest window.

"Course, Precious. Wouldn't be New Orleans if it weren't raining."

"This Krotz is a racist, Sally. Used to was the Big Goofus himself of the Holy Order of Everlasting Yahoos. What's in it for us?"

The deceased senator's widow kneaded her amour's tight little milk chocolate shoulders and said, "Man runnin' his campaign's an old D.C. warrior, hon, name of Zvatiff Thziz-Tczili. Zvatiff helped out Bingo lots of times, special most on the baitfish bill. Remember the scandal when Buster Bustelo, junior senator from New Mexico, was caught with a ten-year-old Vietnamese girl in a Baltimore hotel room?"

"Not really."

"Well, that was Zvatiff's setup. Buster wasn't a bad guy, but he wanted too much in exchange for the use of White Sands as a nuclear waste dumping ground. He was going to kill Bingo's baitfish bill in committee unless Bayou Enterprises deposited a half-million dollars in a numbered Swiss account. It was really the limit. I mean, it's one thing to be dirty, it's another to be that greedy. So Bingo went to Thziz-Tczili, and the old Bulgarian took care of it."

Presciencia rolled over onto her back and looked up at Sally Blaine.

"You've got great tits, Sal. Wish mine were bigger."

Sally laughed, bent over, and kissed Precious gently on the lips.

"You've got a greater commodity, darlin', one that won't shrivel up or fall, neither. Your vision's bigger than anyone's."

"What did Bingo have to do for this Bulgarian?"

"Made sure Louisiana exempted imported sardines from state tax."

"Politics ain't for them that's weak in the stomach, Sal, I know. What's this Klarence Krotz think I could do for him?"

"I'm sure he means to try to get the endorsement of the

Church of the Ungrateful. He needs more than the white vote to get elected. He'll want to stand next to you on the broadcasts."

"Forget it," said Presciencia, sitting up, forcing Sally to dismount. "The No Chingues guys wouldn't let it happen. They'd stomp him."

Sally Blaine shook a Belair menthol from a pack on the bed table, struck a match to it, and inhaled deeply.

"Presh," she said, exhaling, "don't set your mind. Might be we'll need a favor of the sardine man down the line. Life's full of fancy surprises, and some not so fancy, a bunch of which not even you can pick up on in advance. Let's just let it play. What is it James says about people being friends or enemies?"

" 'Know ye not that the friendship of the world is enmity with God? Whosoever therefore will be a friend of the world is the enemy of God.' "

"That's it. And didn't both John and Matthew say, 'You will gain a greater Friend'? Give these folks a chance, pet. By the way, you got a title yet for that book you're writin' about your father?"

"I'm thinkin' of callin' it *He Tasted Death for Me*. From Romans."

Sally smoked and nodded, then said, "I like it, Presh. It's got the nasty ring of truth."

At 6:10, Sally and Presciencia presented themselves at the door of room 603 at the Monteleone Hotel on Royal Street. It was the candidate himself who greeted the two women.

"Miz Blaine, Miz Espanto, please come in. This is a very great pleasure."

Seated in an armchair near the windows was Zvatiff Thziz-Tczili. The corpulent veteran of politics and pederasty did not stand, merely raised his left hand slightly as Klarence placed the visitors together on a red silk–covered love seat. Krotz

48

offered them drinks, which they declined, and then deposited himself in a plush wing chair opposite Zvatiff, facing the women.

"It's a pleasure and an honor, Miz Espanto, to meet you," Klarence said. "I'm an ardent viewer of your broadcasts. May I add, also, that you are even more attractive in person than on television."

Presciencia did not return Klarence's smile. She looked into Krotz's deep-set yellow-blue eyes and saw rows of buildings burn and collapse. She stood up.

"You must pardon me, Mr. Krotz," said the prophetess, "but I cannot stay."

Presciencia walked out of the room without a word to or a glance at Sally Blaine, who remained in the love seat. Klarence sat perfectly still, staring after Precious.

"Don't worry," said Sally, "she just gets nervous sometimes."

"Miz Espanto's a special type person," Klarence said. "Sensitive. I don't take it personal."

"That's up to you, Mr. Krotz."

Beyond Ontology

TYRONE ATREVIDO had followed Presciencia Espanto from Albuquerque to Baton Rouge. Tyrone was one of the members of the No Chingues Con Nosotros attached to the prophetess as a bodyguard. He had accompanied her with Sally to the meeting at the Monteleone, waited in the hotel corridor, and when Precious walked out of the room, Tyrone trailed her.

There were times when Precious simply wanted to walk anonymously through the streets. Her gift of seeing had also become a burden of sorts. She occasionally needed to shed the self she had allowed to form, this being the creation from which the girl Presciencia Espanto felt detached. It was, she realized at these moments, a recognition of control, of the loss of her ability to act spontaneously. Walking out of the hotel room just now had been necessary to maintaining her sanity.

As Tyrone followed closely behind La Preciosa, his five-foot-eight-inch, 280-pound body demanded most of the sidewalk space. He had no idea where she was going and he did not ask. Tyrone's role was to make certain no harm befell the prophetess, and to that purpose he carried two handguns— a matched pair of pearl-handled Colt Pythons—three hand grenades, and a Tanto boot knife.

Grenades were Tyrone's specialty. At one time he had worked for the Albuquerque post office and heard through the grapevine that he was about to be laid off. The next day Tyrone placed two grenades in his lunch box and opened it on his supervisor's desk. "Lay me off," he told his superior, "and I'll blow you up." Tyrone was not laid off, but he was subsequently arrested and charged with intent to commit bodily harm and/or murder and attempted blackmail. He plea-bargained the beef down to possession of a deadly weapon and spent eleven months in the Bernalillo County lockup. Tyrone emerged from jail a legend with a new nickname: El Detonador, the detonator. Since that time, Tyrone had been considered the most dangerous man among the No Chingues gang. For this reason, he was chosen to protect La Preciosa.

Presciencia stopped at the corner of Canal and Carondelet and bought a *Times-Picayune*. She tucked it under her arm and walked up the street and into the Palm-of-the-Hand Coffee Shop, where she took a seat at the counter. Tyrone entered right behind Precious and sat down in a booth by the door. On the table in the booth was a plastic sign that read, THIS TABLE RESERVED FOR TWO OR MORE CUSTOMERS ONLY. A waitress came over and pointed to the sign.

"Sorry, babe," she said to Tyrone. "Unless you expectin' comp'ny, y'all'll hafta sit at the counter."

Tyrone took out a grenade and set it down on the table.

The waitress, who was about forty years old and had had the dubious privilege of serving the motley citizenry of New Orleans for the better part of two decades, clucked her tongue and sighed hard.

"There's necessarily exceptions to every rule," the waitress said. "What'll it be?"

At the counter, Precious ordered tea and lightly buttered rye toast and unfolded the newspaper. On the lower right of the front page she read a heading, ASTRONOMERS TO STOP STARS FROM TWINKLING. The dateline was Apache Point, New Mexico, and the dispatch wire was SNS, the Southern News Service. The prophetess knew that to believers, SNS stood for Satan Never Sleeps. It was through wire reports picked up by newspapers and magazines all over the world that the Satanists issued coded communiqués. She read the brief article.

"A device originally constructed for antimissile defense may be utilized to eliminate the twinkling of stars, long the bedevilment of astronomers. Unlike conventional telescopes, which use stationary mirrors to collect and focus light from celestial objects, this instrument will be equipped with reflectors capable of being continuously deformed by electrically propelled actuators to compensate for distortions caused by twinkling.

"The initial impetus behind such a design was to devise a means of sending laser weapon beams through the atmosphere without dissipating their energy by superfluous reflection. Dr. Alucard Norsk, who plans to install and test the instrument on a 3.5-meter-diameter telescope being built at Apache Point, N.M., said, 'We will be able to observe dust storms on Mars, and analyze the structure of the outer atmospheres of brilliant starbodies. Most of all, we hope to develop adaptive optics as one of the most powerful tools astronomy has ever seen.' "

Presciencia picked out key words in the article: ELIMINATE DEVIL DEFORM DISTORT DEVISE WEAPON POWERFUL TOOL. Her tea and toast arrived and she stopped reading. The quest to construct and to control doomsday machinery was never-ending, as was the struggle against Satan's stalwarts, who were legion. Precious licked the butter off her toast. Evil came in all forms and from all sides, she knew, and now the devil's darts flew faster than ever and from further away. La Preciosa closed her eyes and saw several sleek silver projectiles pierce a quivering lavender veil. She spread her legs slightly to facilitate the flow of her secretions, then bit into the hard bread.

*T*HE *G*OSPEL
*A*CCORDING TO *D*

*I*N THE PRISON LIBRARY, where he had worked for several months, Ice D had read in S. W. Harman's book, *Hell on the Border*, about Rufus Buck, a black outlaw whose band of desperadoes terrorized Oklahoma and Arkansas during the middle part of the last decade of the nineteenth century. Buck and four members of his gang—Lewis and Lucky Davis, Sam Sampson, and Maoma July—were apprehended in August of 1895 and taken to Fort Smith, Arkansas, where they were formally charged with raping a white woman named Rosetta Hassan. Buck's band had been hunted by a force of hundreds of men, including whites, Indians, and blacks. The outlaws' trail of terror encompassed rape, residential burglary, horse theft, and highway robbery. Four women in all were violated sexually, one of them an Indian girl, who died. The white women survived and testified at the trial.

Ice D, whose reading matter heretofore had been limited to comic books and karate magazines, had heard El-Majik refer in one of his speeches to the "frame-up" and subsequent execution of Rufus Buck and his men as an unjust action by whites against blacks. When a copy of *Hell on the Border* fell to the floor from one of the library carts, Ice D picked it up and the name Rufus Buck caught his eye. According to the author, Buck's crimes, D learned, had been perpetrated on persons of all races; when it came to victims, the man did not discriminate. The convict began to suspect that El-Majik was not above manipulating the facts of history for his own purposes.

An item Ice D found fascinating was a strange poem Rufus Buck had written just before his execution on the back of a photograph of his mother he had always carried with him. Decorated with a cross and a drawing of Jesus Christ, the farewell poem impressed Ice D in a way he could not properly explain, even to himself. He had copied it from the book and kept it with him ever since. Before falling asleep in a cardboard box under a stairwell in an abandoned building on LaSalle Street the night he and Spit stole the pistols, Ice D lit a match and studied the poem for perhaps the fiftieth time.

My, dream,—1896
I, dreampt, I was, in, heaven,
Among, the, angels, fair;
i'd, near, seen, non, so handsome,
that, twine, in, golden, hair;
they, looked, so, neat, and, sang, so, sweet
and, play'd, the, golden, harp,
i, was, about, to pick, an angel, out,

and, take, her, to my, heart;
but, the, moment, i, began, to plea,
i, thought, of, you, my, love,
there, was none, i'd, seen, so, beautifull,
on, earth, or heaven, above,
good, bye, my, dear, wife, and. mother
all. so. my. sisters
RUFUS BUCK
Youse. Truley

I Day. of. July
Tu, the, Yeore
off
1896

H
O
L
Y
Father Son
G
H
O
S
T

virtue & resurresur. rection.
Remember, Me, Rock, Of, Ages

How could a man, black, white, or brown, D wondered,
do such terrible things as Rufus Buck apparently did, and
then express himself in such tender fashion? Ice D hunkered
down in the box and closed his eyes. He could hear Spit
Spackle snoring and groaning in his sleep in another box on
the other side of the stairwell. The stench of stale vomit,
rotting garbage, and urine invaded D's nasal passages and he
fought against the nausea that threatened to overwhelm him.
He had forgotten now whether Rufus Buck had been hanged
or shot to death by a firing squad. Had Buck been set up, as

El-Majik claimed, or had he committed those heinous acts? In the middle of the night, the fugitive had come to believe, either nothing made sense or everything did. It was in daylight that confusion reigned and the most terrible behavior took place. This was because darkness covered the planet most of the time and was the most natural state. Light became the border between night and night, and it was always, D decided, hell on the border.

ALMOST PERFECT

SPIT AND ICE D moved slowly through the crowd at the Krotz rally in the parking lot of the Lion's Hall in Jefferson. The candidate had not yet appeared on the platform but Spit spotted El-Majik and his fellow demonstrators making their way toward the stage.

"Catch that, D," Spackle whispered to his partner. "We got two birds and two sets o' stones."

"Got that right," Ice answered, unsmiling, seeing his former mentor. "Gon' be mo' 'nough, bro. Mo' 'nough."

The evening air was wet and sticky but both escapees felt cool. When Klarence Kosciusko Krotz jumped up in front of them, the assembled white trash went wild, whistling, shouting, and applauding. Crushed among them was Cleon Tone, who had positioned himself perfectly to accomplish his self-ordained mission, next to the speakers' platform. Krotz waved at the people, leaned toward the microphone, and spoke into it:

" 'Judge me, O Lord; for I have walked in mine integrity. I have trusted also in the Lord; therefore I shall not slide.' "

"You ain slidin', but you dyin'!" shouted D, as he fired up into the face of the former Great and All-Powerful Grand Beast, tattooing him with three bullets in the forehead: one each for the Father, the Son, and the Holy Ghost.

Confusion ensued, and as the mob milled, D faded back into it. Spit snuck up behind the suddenly isolated El-Majik, the black separatist's entourage straining forward to see what had happened, and popped him twice, once each into the lambda and obelion. Spit, too, quickly withdrew and headed for the meeting place that he and D had agreed upon prior to the rally. Neither of the assassins encountered any difficulties while making their respective getaways.

The Reverend Tone stood in his place, stunned. He had not even removed his pistol from his coat pocket. Soon Tone found himself walking along LaBarre Road, headed toward the river. He went into a Quik Stop, bought a can of Sterno, a loaf of Wonder bread, a box of Blue Diamond matches, and an orange plastic cup decorated with the logo of the New Orleans Saints football team. Cleon continued to River Road, where he sat down, stripped open the Sterno, heated it with the use of a half-dozen matchsticks, then poured the liquid through three pieces of white bread into the Saints cup. Before drinking the contents, the fallen minister, his design of absolution destroyed, intoned aloud, " 'Lord, I have loved the habitation of thy house, and the place where thine honor dwelleth. Gather not my soul with sinners, nor my life with bloody men in whose hands is mischief, and their right hand is full of bribes. But as for me, I will walk in mine integrity:

redeem me, and be merciful unto me. My foot standeth in an even place: in the congregations I will bless the Lord.' "

Later that night, Tyrone Atrevido, driving Presciencia Espanto and Sally Blaine along River Road toward the Huey P. Long Bridge, saw the crumpled dark form that was the collapsed preacher and stopped the car. Tyrone got out and examined the body.

"Is he alive?" asked Precious, peeking over her Ray-Bans.

"He's breathing, but barely," reported Tyrone.

"Put him in the car," ordered the prophetess.

"Sí, La Preciosa."

On a bus headed southeast out the St. Bernard Highway, at Violet, a young white man wearing a Walkman who was seated directly behind Croesus Spackle and Demetrious Youngblood leaned forward and said to them, "You fellas hear 'bout the killin's?"

"No," said Spit, not turning around. "What killin's?"

"Krotz, one runnin' for gov'nor. Him an' El-Majik, come to heckle, both murdered over at the rally in Jefferson. Krotz's campaign manager, man from Sardinia or somewhere, died, too. Heart attack. Heard it just now on the tubes."

"It's a violent world we livin' in," Spit said. "Ain' a body safe, I reckon."

" 'The wicked walk on ev'ry side, when the vilest men are exalted,' " said the young man.

"Amen," said Spit. "What you think, D? What you think the shape the world?"

Ice D looked out the window at the ghostly moonlit trees flashing by.

"Baby," he said, "it's almos' poifec'."

RUN TO EVIL

THE ISLEÑOS came from the Canary Islands to Louisiana in 1778 and settled on Delacroix Island, a spit of land at the eastern tip of St. Bernard Parish. The Isleños persevered despite repeated hurricanes and floods, and the families that remained were able to forge a living by trapping—mostly muskrats—during the late-fall and early-winter months, and fishing and crabbing the rest of the year. The clannishness of the Isleños is well known, and virtually all of the residents of Delacroix are related by blood or marriage. The entire population of the island—which is not really an island, except, perhaps, in cultural terms—has never numbered more than fifty or sixty since the 1930s.

It was unusual, therefore, when Tombilena Gayoso, who had been born and raised at Delacroix before running off to

61

New Orleans when she was seventeen, returned to the island four years later with a husband, Pace Roscoe Ripley, and reestablished with him her life among the Isleños. Ripley, who was in his mid-forties, joined Tombilena's father, Rodrigue, and her brother, Campo, in the crabbing business, and also assisted them in the operation of a small bar they owned at land's end called Tommy's, named after Tombilena.

Pace and Tombilena lived on a houseboat painted "haint" blue, a popular color in south Louisiana, believed by many to keep spooks from entering the domicile. Though Pace had traveled widely during his lifetime—he had been born in North Carolina, raised mainly in the New Orleans area, and lived in Nepal, New York, and Los Angeles—he enjoyed the closeness of the Isleño community, even though he knew he would never be accepted completely by them. Tombilena's father and brother needed another hand, however, so they made Pace welcome. The Gayoso mother, Feroza, had died of emphysema—she had smoked four packs of unfiltered Lucky Strike cigarettes every day for twenty years—six months after Tombilena's departure, and the men were glad to again have a woman among them.

When Spit and Ice D appeared early one morning at the door of Tommy's, Pace sensed trouble. Campo, Pace thought, called white with black "piano keys."

"Sorry, boys," Pace said to them from behind the bar, "we don't open until five in the afternoon."

The men came in anyway.

"You open now, looks like," said D.

"I'm just cleaning up. Come back later, if you want."

"You own a boat?" asked Spit.

"My wife's family does. I don't."

The two cons pulled out their guns.

"Let's get it," said Spit. "We need you to take us some-where."

"Where might that be?"

"Belize."

"We wouldn't get that far. It's just an old crab boat."

"Let's try," Spit said.

"Try this," said Tombilena Gayoso Ripley, who stood in the doorway holding a double-barreled Savage shotgun loaded with number four shot. She tossed her head so that her long, glistening black curls did not obstruct her vision. She pointed the weapon at the two strangers.

"Fuck you, bitch," said D.

Tombilena blasted him first. His head exploded, splattering Spit with blood, brains, and bone. Spit actually tried to shoot back, but the second shotgun shell shattered his auriculo-infraorbital plane before the index finger of his gun hand had received the relay.

Pace poked his head up from behind the bar and saw his wife still standing in the doorway, smoke curlicuing out of the Damascus barrels of the fifty-year-old Savage.

" 'Their feet run to evil, and they make haste to shed in-nocent blood,' " said Tombilena.

"I'm with that good ol' boy from Ferriday on this one," said Pace.

"Who's that?"

"Jerry Lee Lewis. He said, 'I'm too weak for the Gospel. I'm a rock 'n' roll cat.' "

They both laughed.

SMART MOUTH

"GOOD EVENING, PEOPLE, and welcome to *Prostitutes Talk to Christ*. I'm your host, Roland Rocque, the Smartest Mouth in the Deepest South, and if you are a regular listener you know by now that opinions expressed on this program do not necessarily reflect the views of radio station WJEW or its sponsors. If you haven't tuned in to us before, well, now you know.

"It's one minute past midnight here in Kenner, Louisiana, and we're broadcasting from the studios of WJEW, located on Airline Highway, one-quarter mile from the New Orleans International Airport. We afford an opportunity to the denizens of the seamy side of life who work in the area to stop by between tricks and give voice to the Lord via the airwaves.

Prostitutes Talk to Christ is strictly nondenominational and open to hookers of every race and sex whether or not either can be satisfactorily determined and/or verified by medical science. Listeners are invited to call in with their comments to our free access line. Here's the number: 1-800-555-WJEW. That's 1-800-555-9539.

"Okay, folks, here's our first guest of the night. Come right in and have a seat. There you go. Well, that's a conscience-raisin' outfit you have on. My! Lavender taffeta, isn't it?"

"Yeah, Rolan', it is."

"And your first name is? No last names on the air, please."

"Rosetta, from Sicily Isl', Louisiana."

"What is it you must tell Jesus, Rosetta?"

"Well, Rolan', firs' off I jus' wants to thank you fo' what you doin'. Givin' this oppatunity to airwave our inmost religious thoughts an' all."

"Rosetta, it's our pleasure and your choice."

"Righ', okay. I ain' rehearse nothin' now, you know."

"Don't be shy, dollin'. Go ahead."

"Lord, if you be listen, please unnastan' I wouldn' be doin' no nastiness 'less it necessary feed my babies, which there be two: Oprah Winfrey an' Paula Abdul, twin girls. They three now."

"How old are you, Rosetta? If you don't mind my askin'."

"Nineteen, Rolan'."

"And you've been working as a prostitute for how long?"

"Fo' years, almos'."

"Speak to Jesus, Rosetta."

"Jesus, I don' do no drug. I ain' never wan' my babies be strung up on the dope. Pressure be bad, though. Prince Egyp', he my man, he like his ladies go fo' it. Keep 'em control, you know. But Jesus, I tryin' keep my min' straight.

I aks you an' yo' daddy hep me an' my babies stay off it. Gi' me the strength, Jesus, resis'. That all I aks, Rolan'. Let me do my job without no jones."

"Thank you, Rosetta. I'm sure Jesus hears you. And if any of you out there in the Greater New Orleans area are hearin' Rosetta and have a thing to say, call in: 1-800-555-WJEW. That's 1-800-555-9539. I see the lines lightin' up already, Rosetta. You bein' hoid."

"Maybe one of 'em be Jesus, Rolan'."

"That wouldn't surprise me, Rosetta. One day pick up and there's the Son of God himself on the line. Let's take this one. Hello, this is Roland Rocque, the Smartest Mouth in the Deepest South, with Rosetta on *Prostitutes Talk to Christ.* Who's this?"

"Roland? You do better for that nigger whore just shoot her and her babies, too. Put 'em straight out they mis'ry. They just livin' off the good folks, folks right with God and country to begin with."

"Sir, I'm endin' you right now. Sorry, Rosetta, that's not typical of our listenin' audience, I know."

"That okay, Rolan'. I know what kinds peoples is roamin' free. They pays me let 'em come on my face, then go home to they wife 'cross the lake."

"Next caller, I hope you more enlightened than the last one."

"That was terr'ble, Roland. It's callers like him should be shot, not degraded victims of society such as little Rosetta there. It was up to me, anyone who wasn't in church on Sunday doesn't have a good goddam reason they shouldn't be deported. Send 'em to China, be force' to speak Chinese, nothin' but rice to eat, wear them plain-lookin' clothes. What you think, Roland?"

"I think it's time for a break here, Rosetta, pay some bills.

I know you gotta get back on the street, sweetheart, so I want to thank you for comin' on the air tonight."

"Be my pleasure, Rolan'. Can I come back?"

"Certainly, Rosetta, any time."

Pace Ripley sat in a wicker chair on the deck of his houseboat in Delacroix, smoking a joint and listening to the radio. His wife, Tombilena Gayoso, came out, looked at the water shimmering in the moonlight, stretched her arms over her head, and yawned.

"You comin' to bed, Pace?"

"In a few minutes, Tommy. I'm listenin' to this call-in show, *Prostitutes Talk to Christ*. You wouldn't believe the shit people say."

"Mostly that's all people do say, is shit. Bein' more'n twice my age you must surely have noticed that by now."

Pace flicked his roach over the railing.

"Roland Rocque got nothin' on you in the smart mouth department, I'll go that far."

"Come inside, babe, you can go as far as you like. I won't stop you."

She switched off the radio. Pace stood up and took her in his arms.

"Guess I'd better, before you bring out that old shotgun of yours."

Pace kissed Tombilena softly on the lips. She put her right hand on his crotch and giggled as she felt him get hard.

"Am I scarin' you, mister?"

"Honey, can't you tell? I'm petrified."

SHADOW BANDS

THE WHITE STRETCH LIMOUSINE semicircled on the shells in front of Tommy's Bar and stopped. Tyrone cut off the engine and got out. He looked around and scoped nothing moving other than a small, blueish mutt without a tail half-trotting around the channel side of the white wood building, its late-afternoon snooze having been rudely disrupted by the vehicle's intrusion. Tyrone opened the left rear door and Presciencia Espanto stepped out into the weak gray light. A chain of cumulus clouds extended over the region, threatening rain but producing none for the past several days. It was mid-August and south Louisiana was unusually cool and dry.

"Come out, Cleon," Precious said. "Check this place out."

From behind her sunglasses, the sky looked almost brown.

The Reverend Tone, feeling better than he had in ten years following months of tender, loving care from the hands and body of La Preciosa, and dressed in a proper blue suit, emerged from the limo and stood next to her. Cleon had not had an alcoholic drink since being rescued from his Sterno funk by Precious. She had insisted on taking him home with her to Baton Rouge, and within two weeks they had become lovers. Sally Blaine, quite naturally, became insanely jealous and demanded that Precious choose between her and the fallen pastor. When Precious refused to expel Cleon, Sally left on an extended vacation, telling her that she would return only after the prophetess regained her senses.

Precious saw something special in Cleon Tone. She had a feeling that this seeming wreck of man, one who had been reduced to the level of a street beggar and worse, was meant to accomplish something great before the expiration of his allotted time on the planet. It was for this reason only, this intuitive certainty, that Precious was willing to risk her own life, of which Sally Blaine had become such an essential component. Cleon Tone had fallen from grace unto her hands, and La Preciosa was determined to heal him, to help him find his way to that special moment. It might, Precious considered, be the very reason that she herself had been chosen. The importance of this gesture made it not matter to her what anyone else thought, including Sally Blaine.

They had come to Delacroix Island to hire a boat to take them to L'Île des Fantômes, an island in the Caribbean that Precious had been told about by a follower of hers named Colt Bisley. Bisley had died of prostate cancer six months before at the age of eighty-eight in Cuernavaca, Mexico, where he had lived for the final decade of his life. Having become largely incapacitated due to a busted hip and two multiply broken legs after falling from a stepladder while attempting to change a faulty light bulb on the top of his Christmas tree when he was eighty-two, Colt Bisley spent much of his time as a shut-in viewing television via a satellite dish. For a half-century, Bisley had worked in New York City as a stockbroker, earning many millions for himself and his clients, and he had retired to Cuernavaca, where he was confident that his savings would sustain him in a comfortable fashion for the years remaining to him. The former stockbroker fell in love with Presciencia Espanto the first time he saw and heard her rebuilt electronically from Baton Rouge and transmitted to his hacienda, and began sending her money immediately.

Not only did Bisley send financial contributions, but he wrote to La Preciosa regularly. She telephoned him soon after his generous support started flowing, and they maintained a relationship in this manner until his death. Colt told Presciencia that the calmest, most beautiful place on earth was the Isle of Phantoms in the French West Indies, so-called, claimed Bisley, because of the presence of zombies on the island. Many of the islands, Bisley said, had zombies among the populations—Haiti, Martinique, Dominica—but the Isle of Phantoms was the mother of them all. This was where the datura plant grew wild and where the narcolepto-hypnotic drug derived from it had been in use for centuries. Only a few hundred people lived on the island, and the only way there was by private boat. Bisley had visited the Isle of Phantoms just once, with a French client aboard a yacht, and regretted never having returned.

Bisley had left two million dollars to the Church of the Ungrateful, and Precious promised herself that one day she would check out this mysterious place. Now that she had undertaken the resurrection of Cleon Tone, it seemed a perfect time. Tyrone had arranged transportation to the island

70

through Pace Ripley, whom he had met in New Orleans. Ripley could not refuse the offer of five thousand dollars, especially during the slack season. Pace met Tyrone, Presciencia, and Cleon at Tommy's Bar, where Tyrone doled the cash out to Tombilena.

Knowing that Campo and Rodrigue's boat would not survive such a trip, Pace had worked out an agreement with Campo's friend Axel Heyst to use Heyst's fifty-two-foot Hatteras. Heyst, a Swedish fisherman, lived at Yscloskey, and was at present laid up with a severe case of lumbago. This affliction, the Swede believed, had been caused by a curse placed on him through a *bruxa* by his Brazilian ex-wife, Furacão, who still sent him death threats thirteen years after their divorce, from her home in Recife. Axel and Furacão's only child, a daughter named Ferida, had died when she was two years old, while Furacão was in church. Axel had fallen asleep and Ferida drowned in her plastic swimming pool in less than six inches of water.

Heyst was pleased to rent out his boat, the chronic lumbago having prevented him from fishing for the past two months. He told Campo that the only way he could foresee recovering from this illness would be for him to go to Recife and murder Furacão. As soon as his back pain eased, Heyst swore to Campo and Pace when they came to get the Hatteras, he was going to do just that. The rental fee would pay for a round-trip airplane ticket from New Orleans to Brazil.

The name of the boat was the *White Dwarf*. Axel Heyst was an amateur astronomer, and he had named her after a class of small, highly dense stars of low luminosity.

"There's a solar eclipse coming," Heyst said from his bed, after he had handed over the ignition key. "Don't try to take the *Dwarf* through the shadow bands."

"What are they?" Pace asked.

"Waves of darkness that fall across the earth just before and after totality. They'll mark the craft for evil."

After they were out of Heyst's house, Pace asked Campo what he thought of the Swede's warning.

"Man got witchcraft on the brain," Campo said. "Death of a child'll do bad things to anybody."

"You think he'll really kill Furacão?"

"I don't know about that, but my guess is, he goes to South America, he don't come back. Make that hex work for real. Bright side is, he does, maybe we get to keep the boat. Say, what you think about those people goin' over this island? Lady wears them dark glasses and the two strange dudes?"

Pace shook his head. "Not sure, Campo. Believe it was Joseph Conrad, though, who wrote, 'You don't take a woman into a jungle without bein' made sorry for it sooner or later.' "

Campo crossed himself, spit into his right hand, and threw it back over his left shoulder.

"Boa sorte, irmao," he said.

"Same to you, brother," said Pace.

72

*P*RESTIDIGITATION

"*Y*OU GONNA BE ALL RIGHT with these people, babe?"
Tombilena Gayoso fiercely contemplated her hus-
band, Pace Ripley, the night before he was to ferry Presciencia
Espanto, Tyrone Atrevido, and Cleon Tone across the Gulf
and down to the Isle of Phantoms.

"That's a question, okay," said Pace. "Tyrone's a stand-up
cat, far's I can tell. Other guy, I don't know nothin' about.
Just that he's a preacher of some kind. And this Espanto
woman is some special creature, you know. We seen her on
TV."

"She's the one worries me. You gonna be with 'em how
long?"

"Eight days altogether. One and some down, five on the

island, one and some back. I'm bringin' lots of readin' material."

"Such as?"

"Thought I'd dip back into Conrad, the novels of his I haven't read. *Victory,* maybe, and *Nostromo.*"

"Conrad who?"

"Joseph Conrad. Guy who wrote *Heart of Darkness,* was made into a great movie about Vietnam called *Apocalypse Now.*"

"That the one where the good-lookin' guy goes batshit in his shorts in a hotel room?"

"That's it. And he wrote *Lord Jim,* too. That was also made into a movie."

"Musta been before my time."

"It was Conrad said, 'Words, as is well known, are the great foe of reality.' "

"Not just words, babe. What're the accommodations?"

"There's some hotel they're all stayin' at. La Chute Céleste, I think, is the name. I'm stickin' with the boat."

"Jesus, honey, for eight days?"

"Oh, Tyrone'll swing on by, hang out. I'll be fine. Like I say, I plan on doin' a lot of readin'."

Tombilena walked over to the bedroom door and shut it. She lifted her dress, pulled down her panties, and dropped them on the floor.

"Better give you somethin' you can show those island girls, then, they can incorporate into their culture."

Pace grinned. "You mean you got a trick left you ain't used yet on me?"

Tombilena lowered her thick black eyebrows and stepped toward her husband like Carmen enflamed. She tugged on Pace's belt, lifted her right knee, and rubbed his crotch with it.

"I never needed no tricks to convince you of my sincerity," she said. "It's just some magic for the heart."

" 'The heart is deceitful above all things, and desperately wicked: who can know it?' Jeremiah, 17:9."

"What's that supposed to mean?"

"Only truth there is is what happens. All that's to go by."

"Cut the shit, buddy, and kiss me. Truth is relative, of which I'm the closest to you."

$\mathcal{T}$HE $\mathcal{T}$EMPEST

BOAT CAPSIZES IN STORM
FOUR FEARED DROWNED—
FAMOUS TELEVANGELIST LOST

Miami, Aug. 6 (SNS)—Hurricane Juana's almost 200-mile-per-hour winds appear to have been responsible for the deaths of four people believed lost overboard during the worst tropical storm on record since 1935, when comparable gusts and waves to 30 feet above median sea level hit the central Florida Keys, killing 400. The hurricane's rapid formation is unparalleled in the history of the U.S. Weather Service.

The U.S. Coast Guard reported finding the *White Dwarf*, a 52-foot Hatteras, capsized in the Gulf of Mexico, approximately 100 miles north-northwest of Pinar del Río, Cuba. The boat had issued a distress signal but was unable to ride out the storm until help arrived.

According to information as yet unconfirmed by the Southern News Service, among the four persons believed to have been aboard the *White Dwarf*—whose home port was listed as Yscloskey, Louisiana, and was apparently bound for L'Ile des Fantômes in the French West Indies—is Presciencia Espanto, a televangelist known to her followers as "La Preciosa."

Ms. Espanto, who based her ministry in Baton Rouge, Louisiana, was once indicted by the federal government in El Paso, Texas, for felonious necromancy, but the charges were later dropped.

ꭵNTERLUDE

THE COLPORTEUR

*H*ELGA GRANDEZA WATCHED from behind the steering wheel of her Chevy Blazer as her husband, Cyril "Big" Grandeza, unlocked the passenger side of his new ruby red Thunderbird and pulled it open for Bitsy Tunc. Bitsy was eighteen, sixteen years younger than Big. Doesn't look a month more'n fifteen, thought Helga, as she witnessed her mate of the past fourteen grin at Bitsy like a no-good hound that had just been hit on the head by a ball peen hammer, close the door carefully after the skinny slut had settled her cellulite-free butt comfortably on the prewrinkled cream leather, then hurry around to the driver's side and get in. When Big gunned the T-Bird, Helga cranked the Blazer and followed him into traffic. No way, she promised herself, was the bastard going to get away with poppin' teenagers, not with their own two issue still in grade school.

Big Grandeza was a colporteur, a Bible salesman, as had been his father and his father's father. Helga and Big had been high school sweethearts at Santa Maria Luisa de San Francisco in Bayou Cobra, Louisiana, and together they had settled down in New Orleans. She had never known another man in the biblical sense, and the possibility of female orgasm was for her merely a rumor. Sexual desire was not a particular concern for Helga. That her boy Big had turned out to be a chaser, however, did unsettle the woman, and she was determined to put a stopper in this Bitsy bottle.

The bright T-Bird cruised out Canal, Helga following four car lengths behind. At Telemachus, Big swung left, drove two blocks to Palmyra, and parked. Helga slipped her Blazer behind a Dodge van and watched her huge husband, who was wearing the green-and-red-checkered jacket she had given him the previous Christmas, and his tiny strumpet enter a Puerto Rican–blue bungalow.

Helga got out of her vehicle, strode to the bungalow, and knocked hard on the front door. Bitsy opened it and Helga, who was a fairly large woman, outweighing the Tunc punk by a good forty or fifty pounds, grabbed a fistful of Bitsy's baby-soft blond hair and flung her aside. Big Grandeza was standing in the doorway of a bedroom, his sport coat off, stunned to see his wife bearing down on him in this supposedly secret den of iniquity.

" 'Marriage is honorable in all,' " yelled Helga, as she advanced, " 'and the bed undefiled: but whoremongers and adulterers God will judge.' "

Helga raised her left hand over her head and Big, seeing that her fingers grasped a serrated-edged, nine-inch-long Ginsu, backed into the bedroom.

"Goddam, Helga!" he shouted. "Put down that fuckin' knife!"

" 'Thou child of the devil, thou enemy of all righteousness, wilt thou not cease to pervert the right ways of the Lord?' "

Bitsy picked herself up off of the pink pile carpet and bolted out the front door, choking on her own vomit as she ran.

Big took up an antique lamp from a side table, a faux Tiffany that Hubert Tunc had paid way too much for after his wife, Floyda, had bugged him to bid on it at a furniture auction in Nashville five years before. Big hurled it at the enraged Helga, missing her, and the expensive missile exploded against a bureau, its dubious value reduced by all. Helga charged and Big cringed, curling up on the floor like a sow bug.

His furious spouse's weapon penetrated the back of Big's neck like a cleanly placed *muleta*. The colporteur groaned and pitched sideways, his blue tongue wagging, rivulets of blood draining from both mouth and nostrils. Helga sat down heavily on the bed, perspiring as she had not at any time in her life save during the act of childbirth.

" 'To the one we are the savor of death unto death,' " she said, panting between words, " 'and to the other the savor of life unto life. And who,' " asked the murderess, " 'is sufficient for these things?' "

WALK

Mother of God

$\mathcal{F}$OLLOWING THE DEATH of her husband, Pace Ripley, who was lost at sea and believed drowned during a hurricane, Tombilena Gayoso, age twenty-eight, childless, had relocated from Delacroix Island, Louisiana, to New Orleans. Though only forty-five minutes by car from her family—her father, Rodrigue, and brother, Campo, were fishermen in Delacroix—N.O. was, to borrow a phrase from the Rolling Stones, two thousand light-years from Tombilena's home. She felt the need to change her life after Pace slipped away, and a shift to the Crescent City, where she had lived previously for a short time—where, in fact, she and Pace had first met—was both a convenient and obvious move. Tombilena was the only Gayoso woman now, her mother having passed several years before, and she wanted to remain within hailing distance of her father and brother, both of whom she loved dearly.

In short order, Tombilena found an apartment at the edge of the Quarter above a bookshop on the corner of Barracks and Dauphine; and a part-time job answering calls at the Mary Mother of God Rape Crisis Center on Terpsichore Street. Established by women united in the belief that the mother of Jesus Christ, the so-called Virgin Mary, actually had been a rape victim, the Mary Mother of God organization functioned as an all-purpose assistance service for women burdened by any manner of difficulty. Tombilena dealt with the battered, the homeless, the assaulted, and psychologically adrift distaff of the Greater New Orleans area, the numbers of which, to her horror, were legion.

Also present at the center was a sixteen-year-old girl named Marble Lesson. A legend among radical feminists the world over, Marble's notoriety stemmed from her having shot to death the infamous Mozo de Estoques, an international terrorist and assassin, who had attempted to rape Marble when she was fourteen. Following this incident, which took place at a rural airfield near Cuba, Alabama, the teenager had been counseled by several of the women who were then in the process of forming the Mary Mother of God group. After a failed attempt to live in harmony with her mother and stepfather in Florida, Marble Lesson had come to live with her father, a construction worker named Wesson Lesson, in N.O., where she resumed her association with Mary Mother of God.

It was in the company and under the tutelage of these women that Marble developed her political and social manifestos. She read extensively those historical and philosophical texts that her helpmates made available to her, including the writings of Hilda Brausen, a German woman who had disguised herself as a man in order to fight at the front in World

War I. Killed in France during a firefight—some believed by members of her own unit who had discovered Hilda's secret—Fräulein Brausen advanced a fundamental belief that all men were prone to a mental illness that expressed itself in the form of violence toward women. "The male human," Hilda Brausen wrote, "almost invariably will sooner or later be overcome by this disease, and therefore bears close scrutiny, so that at the first sign of derangement he can—and *must*—be eliminated. As grows the male prostate gland, so grows his proclivity for behavior dangerous to the female human."

Though medically unsound, this correlative theory of Hilda Brausen's was nevertheless embraced by an ever-growing number of feminist thinkers. Basing it on "the Brausen principle," Marble Lesson had created a radical faction within Mary Mother of God dedicated to the eradication of any man believed by their society to be guilty of exceptional abuse. This faction, informally called "Die Brausenkriegers," dealt literal deathblows to those men deemed diseased. They eschewed any possibility of rehabilitation.

Tombilena noticed that despite her youth, Marble Lesson was accorded inordinate respect and treated with the utmost deference by the other members of Mary Mother of God. Tombilena's own history was not devoid of violence—she had shotgunned down two men who were threatening to murder her husband—and from what information she could at this point gather about Marble, she thought that the two of them might prove not incompatible.

MALA SORPRESA

$\mathcal{C}$OMBILENA CAME to work at the Mary Mother of God Rape Crisis Center and found the following item, clipped from that morning's newspaper, tacked to the central bulletin board:

FISHERMEN CHARGED
IN RAPE CASE

NEW ORLEANS, June 21 (SNS)—Six men were taken into custody late Saturday night in Delacroix by Louisiana State Police and charged with aggravated battery, false imprisonment, assault with a deadly weapon, and rape with a foreign object.

The men, all of whom are fishermen and residents of the largely Isleño community of Delacroix Island, were arrested in Tommy's Bar following a complaint lodged earlier in the evening by a woman whose name is being withheld.

According to the complaint, it is alleged that each of the men took turns torturing and sexually assaulting the woman with pool cues while the others observed. Each of the alleged perpetrators has denied the charges.

Currently being held in the St. Bernard Parish jail pending bail hearings are: Poco Herida, 26; Naufragio Yema, 18; Campo Gayoso, 24; Valer La Pena, 22; Gallo Viudo, 46; and Sapo Feo, 28.

Reading her brother's name made Tombilena's stomach turn. She felt faint, which she never had before, and quickly sat down in one of the lemon yellow plastic chairs in the waiting room, directly in front of the bulletin board. Marble Lesson entered from the inner office and sat down next to her. She took Tombilena's left hand, the one closest to her, in both of her own.

"We got to talk," said Marble.

MARBLE LAYS IT ON THE TABLE

AFTER TOMBILENA HAD FINISHED SPEAKING on the telephone to her father, Rodrigue, and learned that Campo's bail had been set at fifty thousand dollars, as it had for each of the accused, and that Rodrigue was about to put up the Gayoso house as collateral, she walked with Marble Lesson over to Tallulah's, a café on Religious. Tombilena was still stunned by the news of her brother's alleged involvement in the assault, and she hardly noticed when a waitress brought to their table the cups of coffee Marble had ordered for them.

"Your brother been known to be knockin' females around?" Marble asked, as she stirred a spoonful of brown sugar into her own cup.

Marble was short, about five foot one, with straight, sandy brown hair chopped off under the ears and bangs below her eyebrows. She wore schoolboy glasses that made her greenish blue eyes look even tinier than they were. Her lips were light pink, the same color as her cheeks. Tombilena looked at Marble bringing the cup to her mouth and was startled by how small the girl's fingers were. The sight reminded her of an old movie she and Pace had watched once on TV, *The Incredible Shrinking Man;* the scene where the guy who's fading away due to an undetermined malady is drinking coffee with a lady midget and they're both holding enormous saucers and bowl-like cups in their child-sized hands. It is shortly thereafter that the man, who has come to believe that the shrinking process has ceased, realizes to his horror that it's started again; suddenly, he's smaller than the lady midget. At this moment, Tombilena felt tiny, tinier than she had ever felt before in her adult life.

"I guess I don't really know," she said. "Campo's five years younger'n me, and I ain't closely kept up on his activities these last few years. I was livin' here in N.O. before I got married, then me and Pace, my husband who's now deceased, was mostly concerned with each other. Bein' back in Delacroix, of course, I seen a lot of Campo, but I never heard about nothin' extra strange in his behavior."

Marble took out a pack of Delicado cigarettes and stuck one in her mouth.

Mind if I smoke?" she asked, then before Tombilena could answer, lit it with an inch-and-a-half flame from a freshly polished Zippo that had two Oriental characters engraved on one side.

"What're them scratchin's on your lighter?"

Marble exhaled a bluish stream of Mexican smoke, looked quickly at her fire source, smiled, and dropped it back into the left breast pocket of her red sateen cowboy shirt. Because her breasts were so small, Marble never wore a brassiere, and she liked to feel the cool, smooth weight of the silver lighter against her body.

"Name of a Japanese girl, Take Ahike. She sent it to me from Japan. Writin's called *kanji*, she told me. Chinese, but the Japanese use it. She come to Mary Mother of God with her problem. Man much older'n her—Take was eighteen at the time—he maybe been forty or so, was her cousin, kept her prisoner in his house over in Gentilly Terrace. Love slave stuff. She come to New Orleans to attend the Pillara Salt Memorial Bible College, and her folks back in Osaka had thought they were doin' right arrangin' for her to board with their relative. Man owned a porcelain repair shop on Melpomene and South Tonti."

"He got her pregnant, I guess."

"Never even enrolled her at the college. Kept her locked in a soundproof bedroom for fourteen months. Made her write letters home sayin' how good she was doin' at school and how gracious a host their cousin was."

"How'd she escape?"

"Stabbed him through the right eye with a chopstick one night when he brought her supper. Man would watch her eat, then, before she could finish, Take said, he'd rape her. Seems her chewin' excited him so much he couldn't wait. Take told us he was like a rabbit, on and off real quick, but he done it to her six, seven times a day, sometimes more, every day, even durin' her period, for fourteen months. She said she woke up the middle of her first night in this country with his dick in her mouth."

"Did she kill him?"

Marble puffed a few times, then stubbed out her cigarette in an ashtray.

"No. Blinded him in the one eye, then run out with hardly no clothes on and no money, of course. Didn't know where

96

she was. Happened Helga Grandeza was drivin' by at just that moment—she lives in that neighborhood—and Helga stopped and picked Take up, brought her directly to Mary Mother of God. We took care of everything, then she went back to Japan."

"Her parents know about what happened? The abortion?"

"Doubt it. Take said her folks'd freak if they did, prob'ly all commit *seppuku* 'cause of the humiliation."

"They could've revenged theirselves."

"Die Brausenkriegers took care of that. We waited till after Take had gone home. Her cousin never even tried to find her, far as we know. We told Take to tell her folks that he'd had a heart attack and died."

"What really happened?"

"Night she left, we paid the man a visit. Tied him down to the bed he'd abused her on and invaded the orifices of his person repeatedly with a variety of power tools. Then, before Take Ahike coulda said *sayonara,* we served him his last meal. One natural guess'll get it."

"Penis sushi."

Marble grinned. "You got a future with this company, Ms. Gayoso, but first we gotta agree on the deal involves your brother."

"Marble, before Die Brausenkriegers go into action, let me talk to Campo, see in fact he participated."

"Observin's same as doin' if he done nothin' try to stop it."

"I'll get the details. Campo won't lie to me."

"All right, Tombilena. They ain't no way these boys is escapin' our attention."

"What about the woman? You know who she is?"

"Victoria China Realito, forty-five, from Port Arthur, Texas. She was in New Orleans settlin' the estate of her brother, a pawnshop operator, who was murdered a while back. She met this one of 'em, Gallo Viudo, in Phil's Lounge on St. Roch, then accompanied him to Delacroix. That's all we know right now. Ms. Realito is under heavy sedation at the Hôtel Dieu. Madonna Kim and Junebug are over there, waitin' on her to counsel."

Tombilena's eyes suddenly watered up, and she said, "Marble, I know you're a lot younger than me, but somehow it seems you're way older. This world's so terrible, but it appears you got better'n a hog grip on things."

Marble reached across the table and clasped Tombilena's trembling hands with her own.

"As Jeremiah said, when he was in the *juzgado:* 'The Lord is with me as a mighty terrible one: therefore my persecutors shall stumble, and they shall not prevail: they shall be greatly ashamed; for they shall not prosper: their everlasting confusion shall never be forgotten. But, O Lord of hosts, that triest the righteous, and seest the reins of the heart, let me see thy vengeance on them: for unto thee have I opened my cause.' There's comfort there."

"Oh, Marble, dear Marble, it's so hard not to suffer."

"I know it, Tombilena. One of the reasons I'm on the planet, help spread the sufferin' around more evenly."

SCREEN TEST

TOMBILENA FOLLOWED THE GUARD into an eight-by-twelve-foot room. The floor was covered with dirty gray linoleum; the cement block walls had been painted pale blue. There was no furniture in the room. The guard told Tombilena to stand directly in front of an eight-foot-high gray metal door with a narrow window cut into it sixty-six to seventy-six inches from the floor. A thick green mesh screen was stapled across the window.

"Wet rat they," said the guard, an obese, clay-skinned man Tombilena guessed to be in his early thirties. Headed for an early death by heart attack, she thought.

The guard wore a yellow inchworm mustache that he constantly petted, as if it were a dozing house cat. Tombilena averted her gaze from him and stared into the green mesh.

"When da priznap, tawk direck dat winda."

Tombilena wiped the palms of her hands down the sides of her dress. A shadow appeared on the other side of the screen.

"Hello, Sis," said Campo.

Tombilena meant to talk but instead she burst into tears.

"C'mon, Tommy, it ain't so tough. Daddy havin' me outta here by tomorra noon, latest."

"I can barely see you," she said.

Campo laughed. "I ain't got no prettier, lately, so you not missin' nothin' new."

"Campo, you're my brother, and I love you. You know that, right?"

"Sure, Sis, of course. I love you, too."

"I just need to know you did this thing."

"Aw, Tommy, we can't talk here. Wait Daddy gets me home, I'll tell ya what happen."

Tombilena tried harder to discern the contours of Campo's face, but it was impossible. She wanted to look into his eyes.

"Babe, tell me straight you was or was not involve direckly."

Campo's head swiveled from right to left to right and down. He rested his stubbled chin on his chest.

"It weren't simple, Tommy. All I can say now is, it weren't simple."

"Tom's up, missy," said the guard.

Campo raised his head and pressed his nose against the screen.

"Be out tomorra, Tommy," he said. "Come by Daddy's."

Before Tombilena could reply, Campo was gone. The fat guard opened the outside door and she passed through it without looking at him.

As the elevator conveying Tombilena descended, she suddenly pictured Campo as he was at six years old, sitting in the late-morning sun on the edge of a dock at Delacroix, his skinny little boy's legs dangling above the water. Stretched across his lap was a dead snake, a thick, black cottonmouth, three feet long. Campo was sawing away at it with a rusty pocketknife, sweating in silence as he attempted to severe the vampirish, venom-filled head. The eleven-year-old Tombilena had stood near her brother and witnessed his fierce concentration. Campo's eyes were hidden, as if they had retracted into secret compartments in his face. He did not look up while his sister was there. The boy worked feverishly, the blood and viscera of the viper spewing forth, spotting and dripping from Campo's forehead, cheeks, chest, and legs. Just as Tombilena's memory bank called forth the cottonmouth's head dropping onto the dock, its bleached fangs gleaming in the glare, the elevator door opened to the ground level of the building and she shuffled forward with the other passengers into the lobby.

Tombilena stood perfectly still for a full minute, sweating as Campo had that day on the dock, waiting for the ugly feeling that had overcome her to pass. It was almost as if the slightest motion on her part might trigger some sanguinary monster into sinking its poisonous teeth into the deepest part of her helpless brain.

*W*HEN *L*IFE *I*S *L*IKE A *C*HEAP *H*OTEL *R*OOM

Dear Jesus,

Well this is sure it. This is letter number 666 that I have written to You over these past few years 666 is the devils number as You well know and I have dreaded coming to it but theres nothing to be done other than show him how his name and number mean nothing to a Believer on the Righteous side so consider this only another letter from me to You. We have a Situation here at Mary Mother of God. There is a problem that I thought it best to share with You before deciding on. One of the women who has come lately to work with us her name is Tombilena Gayoso she is an Isleno as is her brother who participated in an attack on a girl in Delacroix. This girl was raped by six men with poolsticks. A bunch of fishermen not unlike some of the ones You run with back in the days. The difficult part concerns this woman who is among our organization and her desire to spare her brother from the wrath of the Righteous she knows is coming to be visited upon each of these men done the devils work. There was lightning here today Jesus that struck close to the roof of our building out of an anvil-shaped cloud and continued to spark for twenty minutes or more. I was not frightened so much as surprised and impressed by the display of Your Daddys power. Watching the electric sky my mind kinda wandered back to when I was much younger and my Daddy was all the time drunk a time when he would fall in the road any old place even in the path of truck traffic and sleep. People would rescue him and he would not even know later what happened. He recovered and said he was so twisted up in his brain about the divorce from my mother Bird who lives now in Florida that he did not care what befell him. But the difficult decision here is should we let Tombilena deal with her brother herself. I am tempted to let her as a way of testing her commitment to our cause at Mary Mother of God. Die Brausenkriegers as I told you before are already set to take care of the other five in fact before there can be a trial. A good guess is they would leave the country on boats and never have a day in court. I saw on the TV news yesterday about a 6 year old girl who was stole out of her house in the middle of the night. They found the man who done it after he returned her to the home after molesting her in all kinds of ways and had shot the girl up with drugs and burned her body with cigarettes. This man had tattoos one of a lizard on an arm and a skull I think on the other that he cut off after she had told the police about them and this information was printed in the newspaper he must have read it. He had been kidnapping and having sex with girls down to the age of 9 months old Jesus

I sometimes cannot even believe the sickness that is walking around loose out the door. If this is a test of us it is a severe one only You know why. I am thankful to be such a strong young person but I feel older than almost everybody aint that weird? My daddy Wes has fell off the wagon too which is the other terrible news. Last night I discovered him passed out from beer on the front porch so I pulled him inside the house where he woke up and said over and over Im not dyin in some cheap hotel room Im not dyin in some cheap hotel room. Jesus I hate to say this but life can get more awful the more a person sees of it.

Sincerely Your faithful
Marble

WOLVES OF
THE EVENING

"WHAT DO YOU THINK of this as an idea?" said Madonna
Kim Epps at the Tuesday evening executive session
of Mary Mother of God. "You know how there's becomin'
about every type program on cable TV these days? Like the
Comedy Channel, Home Shoppin' Channel, Cartoon Channel, and such. Well, I figure there oughta be the Execution
Channel. For those states such as Utah, Texas, Florida, and
us offers capital punishment, should be they're televised to
the nation. Let everybody see what it's like."

"This is definitely one of your better notions, M.K.," said
Saramel Meridian. "I mean that seriously. Even better would
be to take those scumbuckets stole people's life savin's in the
S and L scandal, and greedy stockbroker robbers, the white-
collar criminals ripped off hundreds of millions from everyone,

and hang 'em on public TV, let 'em twist till there ain't nothin' left but their viscera swayin' in the wind. That way, folks could tune in anytime, day or night, for months, and see what becomes of them's responsible for the starvation and deaths of thousands of poor and disabled people."

"I like it," Madonna Kim said, nodding enthusiastically. "In fact, we ought to consider expandin' our activities to include men like you're talkin' about. Ones ought to be slaughtered 'stead of spendin' a year or two in some minimum security country club and payin' what to them's a diddleyshit fine."

"What else gripes me," said Saramel, "is how they all of a sudden find religion, about which they're sincere as hell, I'm certain."

"Cut this item from the *Times-Picayune* yesterday," Madonna Kim said as she removed a piece of paper from a pocket. "Which is what started me thinkin' in this line. Obituary of Albert Pierrepoint, died at eighty-seven years old, in London."

"Who was he?" asked Junebug Gilliam, putting a match to her Prince Edward stub.

"Public executioner of England for the past twenty-five years. His father and uncle were hangmen, too. Says he sent four hundred thirty-three men and seventeen women to their eternal reward. In a school essay, written when he was twelve, Pierrepoint said, 'I would like to be the public executioner as my dad is, because it needs a steady man who is good with his hands.'"

"Hard to know if he was right thinkin', though," said Saramel. "Prob'ly not."

"Article goes on to say he changed his mind on the deterrent factor of the death penalty after he retired. Course most do before kickin' off. But this is the best part: 'His past never played on his conscience,' said Patricia Wynne, owner of the nursin' home where Albert Pierrepoint died. 'He didn't brood.' "

"We don't neither," said Junebug, enjoying her cigar. "Least, not me."

"I," Madonna Kim corrected her. "Not I."

"Didn't think you did," said Junebug.

Marble Lesson stood up and the room became quiet.

"I've decided to let Tombilena Gayoso take care of her brother in this case," Marble announced. "I'm confident she'll handle the situation to our satisfaction. The others, we'll do."

"Whatever's right," Saramel said, and the others echoed her.

Unbidden, the women rose as one and joined hands in a circle, closing their eyes as they did so. Junebug bit tenderly on the Prince.

Marble spoke: " 'For I have heard a voice as of a woman in travail, and the anguish as of her that bringeth forth her first child, the voice of the daughter of Zion, that bewaileth herself, that spreadeth her hands, saying, Woe is me now! for my soul is wearied because of murderers.'

"Thus spake Jeremiah, who also sayeth: 'Wherefore a lion out of the forest shall slay them, and a wolf of the evenings shall spoil them, a leopard shall watch over their cities: every one that goeth out thence shall be torn in pieces. . . .' Praise Jesus, bless these beasts we embody for the Lord's duty. Amen."

"Amen," chorused the women.

BLACK KISS

$\mathcal{T}$HE NIGHT before Tombilena left for Delacroix, Marble
had handed her a seventeen-shot nine-millimeter Glock
pistol and a copy of *Magnificent Female: An Intimate Memoir
of Hilda Brausen* by Eva von Blutvergiftung, translated from
the German by Irma Zunge.

These items were on the front seat beside Tombilena Gayoso
as she drove east in her Toyota 4-Runner on Louisiana State
Highway 46. Finding herself too agitated to sleep last night,
Tombilena had read several chapters of *Magnificent Female*
before finally falling out for a couple of hours. Eva von Blutvergiftung had been Hilda Brausen's governess from the age
of four until Hilda turned thirteen, at which time Eva, then
in her early thirties, introduced her precocious charge to the
carnal delights of Sapphic culture. This sexual liaison contin-

ued secretly for four years, until the pair were discovered engaged in an act they referred to as "releasing the pythoness" on the pantry floor of the Brausen family summer home in Blindheit by Hilda's father, Bruno. Horrified and enraged, Herr Brausen beat both women with a mop handle so severely that they required hospitilization.

Bruno Brausen, a beer baron whose brewery empire extended from Munich to Mexico City to Shanghai, disowned his seventeen-year-old daughter, casting her into the world with a subsistence-level stipend to be doled out to her by his lawyers only until she reached the age of twenty-one. Those same lawyers brought charges against the woman their client perceived as a heinous corrupter of youth, and succeeded in providing her—subsequent to a highly publicized trial—a six-year prison sentence for the practice of deviant behavior with a child.

It was during her incarceration at the women's penal colony on the island of Schwips that Eva von Blutvergiftung wrote the first part of her memoir. She then set it aside until after Hilda's death. Because of Hilda Brausen's notoriety as a polemicist prior to World War I, and the public controversy that ensued concerning the circumstances of her death, Eva—who had not seen or corresponded with her former lover since the details of their relationship were served up to the masses by the European press in the most scandal-inducing fashion—completed her book, including in it not only material of a personal nature, but an eccentric analysis of female sexual urges and responses later acknowledged by Wilhelm Reich as having proved extremely useful to his research for *The Function of the Orgasm.*

Suppressed by the governments of Germany and Austria for more than a decade following its initial publication in Zurich in 1920, *Magnificent Female* became an international best-seller, and had never been out of print in the German, French, Italian, and English languages during its author's lifetime. Eva von Blutvergiftung died in 1960 in New York City, where she had been the proprietress of a vivarium on Second Avenue that specialized in pythons. She was believed to be at least ninety years old.

Tombilena found the book difficult—in part due to Irma Zunge's stilted and dated translation—but fascinating. Aside from the story of the love affair between the woman and the girl, Eva von Blutvergiftung's copious classifications of sexual dynamics mystified Tombilena. She never knew there was so much to say about fucking. What she did know, she decided, was that reading Eva von Blutvergiftung's exegesis served to suppress in her sexual desire of any kind. Not that she had been up for much these days, anyway, but old Eva, Tombilena thought, was as weird a turnoff as ever there was likely to be.

Tombilena glanced down at the Glock, admired its contours, and lifted it with her right hand. She balanced the gun in her palm as she returned her gaze to the road, then was suddenly startled by the lethal feeling implicit in the pistol's weight. A blackness crept up her arm and Tombilena dropped the weapon onto the seat. She pressed hard the inside of her right wrist against her lips and kissed its heat, then managed to pull the 4-Runner off to the side and kill the engine before blacking out.

SOUVENIRS

"*L*IGHTNIN' TERRIFY YOU, Miss Marble?"

Marble Lesson was visiting Victoria China Realito at Junebug Gilliam's house, where the recuperating rape victim was staying out of the public eye.

"Never been comfortable about it," Marble said, "ever since I was in a Greyhound was struck by it in Mississippi. Bus crashed, killed all the passengers except me. I was fourteen, then."

"After I lost my child by drownin'," said Victoria China, "I drifted for years. Went from one place to another, not really carin' what happened to me. Drank a lot, mostly turkey wine. Then I met a man on the street in West Memphis, Arkansas, straightened me out. Man had been an agronomist before he become a bottle baby. We took up together. One time we was

111

sheltered inside an abandoned buildin' durin' a fearsome storm, and he told me all about how lightnin' helps the crops grow."

Marble, who was seated in a straight-backed wicker chair next to the porch swing Victoria China was stretched out on, studied the woman's face. Blue, black, gray, and red lines decorated the topography like an AAA roadmap of central Illinois.

"Thought that's an old wives' tale," said Marble.

"Ain't. As lightnin' passes through the atmosphere, it converts nitrogen into ammonia, and ammonia helps the plants. Soybeans and locust trees convert nitrogen into ammonia too, same as blue-green algae. Course, any organic matter decomposes in the soil does the same job. It's one of the basic processes creates an environment can support plants and animals both."

"You learn all this from that wino you run with in West Memphis?"

"He's the one sparked my interest in lightnin'. I read up on it some after that. Me and Emil—that was his name, Emil Mooth—had taught at a college up east. Professor of agronomy, I guess. He sure enough knew about plants. We got separated somehow in Helena, Arkansas, it was, and I ain't seen him since."

"Ms. Realito, I just want you to know that we at Mary Mother of God are gonna handle this situation in our own way."

The highways and rivers of Victoria China's face shifted furiously, as if affected by an earthquake of considerable magnitude.

"First scalps got took durin' the French and Indian War," she said. "Frogs forced the savages to do it, keep an accurate count of the kills. What type proof you gals fixin' to bring me?"

DRESS CODE

C AMPO GAYOSO poured himself a third cup of Community coffee, left it black, and sat down at his kitchen table. He let the Patsy Cline tape play a second time. One of his girlfriends, Billy Kate Kimbrough, had brought it over more than a month before and hadn't been by since. "I've got these little things, she's got you," Patsy sang. Old-time country wasn't the kind of music Campo usually listened to, but he had to admit this woman had a natural way of keeping a person's attention. Campo liked things natural, meaning when, where, and what he wanted; and never mind why. Being that this was his first free day since his daddy, Rodrigue, had bailed him out of jail on the rape and aggravated battery beef, Campo contemplated his natural feeling for human contact, picked up the telephone, and dialed Billy Kate's number.

" 'Lo."

"Hey, Miss Billy Kate Kimbrough. You answer this question correctly, you win a trip to Las Vegas, Nevada. AEP."

"What's the letters mean?"

"All expenses paid. Now, why did the blonde get so upset when she got her new driver's license in the mail?"

"Let me think."

"Time's up! She was upset to see she got a F in sex."

"Saint Rose of Lima, Campo, you loose already?"

"Iron bars couldn't hold me, but your arms could."

"That my Patsy Cline tape playin' in the background?"

"Put it on this mornin', thinkin' of you. Want to come get it?"

"Love to, Campo, but I can't. My uncle Rex got arrested five this A.M. for lewd and lascivious behavior over to Violet. I got to go take care of my cousin Connie's kids while she bonds him out."

"What'd her daddy do now?"

"Exposed his self to a raghead clerk at the Kwik-Way. Uncle Rex was wearin' his blue dress."

"Seems it's his favorite garment of late."

"Uncle Rex is forty-six years old and my guess is now he'll have to be committed to Oriental."

"He'll do good, they let him bring his wardrobe. Rex ain't never hurt nobody, has he?"

"Only the tons of mental wreckage he caused his daughter, is all."

"Connie's makin' out. She and Edgar Zarzoso still together?"

"More or less. Lately's less."

"She'd be better off chuckin' that red-ass altogether."

"Edgar ain't partial to Uncle Rex's habits, neither."

"They do got decidedly different taste in clothes."

"This ain't will be a good day for me, Campo, pie. I'm on the runny now, too. Just started."

"Sight of female blood never bothered me, Billy Kate. You know it."

"I do want to hear your side of the story. Maybe I can get away later."

"Call me, or I'll be at the bar."

"Okay, pie. Bye."

Campo hung up. Patsy was wailing away on "Sweet Dreams." He took a sip of coffee and decided to spike it with a shot of Wild Turkey.

Tombilena walked in, saw the bottle in her brother's hand, and said, "I hope you know you got a problem."

Campo laughed, showed a good many of his deteriorating teeth, and poured.

"*Bem-vindo, irmá!*" he said. "I ain't never worn no blue dress, if that's what you mean."

THE FUTURE OF JAZZ

*J*UNEBUG GILLIAM and Marble Lesson stood next to one another in the laundry room at Mary Mother of God, folding clothes they had just extracted from the dryer. Every woman who worked at the center took regular turns doing the chores. Junebug enjoyed folding laundry, she told Marble, because the repetition reminded her of who she was and why she was on the planet.

"The great fault in women is to desire to be like men."

"What?"

"Fortune I got last night in a fortune cookie," said Junebug. "At Tu Luong. Almost didn't pay the bill."

"Point of fact, though, Junie, there ain't no good reason a woman should desire to be like a man. Not that the Chinamen make up them fortunes got any kinda clue, but it's so."

"This mornin' I got up and played an old record belonged to Elton Esto, my second husband. He was a drummer with King Wiggly and His Jazz Rabbits. You're too young, prob'ly, remember 'em."

"What was the record?"

"Thelonious Monk and Johnny Griffin at the Five Spot. That second cut, 'Comin' on the Hudson,' where they just slide ahead and drop a big blue dream down your ear before you know what's happened. Elton Esto used to play it, or 'Bolivar Blues,' when he'd get up, which was usually about two or three in the day. Light a Kool, fix a double Bloody Mary, and by the time he's ready for coffee, there'd be Monk plunkin' on 'Functional.' Elton Esto was mad about Monk in the mornin'. Said his music kept the earth from tippin' all the way over."

"What become of him?"

"Monk? Or Esto?"

"Esto."

"Had a fatal heart attack while he was freebasin' with King Wiggly's wife, Phaedra. They'd been carryin' on behind nobody's back for months. Both Wig and I knew about it, and there was some untidy scenes, but when Phaedra and Esto got torn up on dope, I bailed. Wig forced Phaedra to go through rehab, but it didn't take. She got her throat cut while she was hookin' to buy drugs a year later in Miami. Cops found her drowned in her own blood, four A.M. front of the Hotel Casablanca."

Marble said, " 'Keep me from the snares which they have laid for me. . . . Let the wicked fall into their own nets, whilst that I withal escape.' "

" 'Keep me, O Lord,' " said Junebug, " 'from the hands of the wicked; preserve me from the violent men, who have purposed to overthrow my goings.' "

The women ceased their folding and embraced.

" 'Be not afraid of sudden fear,' " Marble whispered, " 'neither of the desolation of the wicked, when it cometh.' "

"When we gonna go for them men harmed Victoria China?"

"Soon as Tombilena finishes with her brother."

"Think she's capable?"

"It's a serious test, Junie, but I think she'll know the truth and act accordingly."

Junebug held Marble by the shoulders at arm's length and studied her.

"You're a wonder, girl. I don't mind sayin', in my experience, you're the prize pumpkin."

Marble smiled and said, " 'I have walked before thee in truth and with a perfect heart.' "

"Marble, you think the devil got any idea what he's up against at Mary Mother of God?"

"He did," said Marble, "our work wouldn't be close to complicated."

HOME TRUTHS

"OKAY, TOMMY, how it was. This woman, this Vicky, she call herself, was with Gallo Viudo, who he'd met her in N.O. earlier that night. They was both drinkin' in Phil's Lounge on St. Roch when he tol' her how he's from Delacroix, and she say she never been there. So, he say, let's go."

Tombilena and Campo were sitting on the front porch of his house, drinking Mount Gay rum and orange juice. It was clear to Tommy that her brother did not consider this situation to be of the utmost gravity. Campo's willingness to relate the story seemed to her more in the nature of a favor or polite indulgence, rather than the matter of life and death that she knew it to be.

"My guess is Gallo figure he got him showtime. You know,

for later that evenin'. This point, was nothin' complicated about it."

"She come out with Gallo in his car?"

"Truck, yeah. Tan Ford Ranger, his clutch is always goin' out. You need more rum in there, *irmá?*"

"No, thanks, Campo. I'm fine."

Campo sipped his drink.

"So, okay. There she is now, in the bar. We all there, shootin' pool. Poco, Lucky Yema, Valer La Pena, Sapo Feo, me."

"What time is this?"

"Ten, maybe. Maybe a little after. Gallo brings this Vicky. We look at her, woman maybe his age. Nothin' special about it."

"Was she drunk?'

"Not yet, I wouldn't guess."

"She drank with you boys?"

"Pretty steady, yeah. Towards midnight, midnight-half, when things got strange."

"How strange?"

"Tommy, you know, this Vicky, she was lookin' to do business."

"You sayin' Gallo was pimpin' for her?"

Campo nodded, sipped at his glass.

"He maybe had ideas there. Mentioned to Lucky she'd be willin', anybody had the urge and the cash for gash."

"How about you?"

Campo laughed. "Okay, look, here's what happened. I'm at the bar. Next thing I see this Vicky is spread out on the pool table, Sapo's climbin' over her. Nobody's seemin' to mind this is goin' on, certainly not her."

"Gallo take Sapo's money?"

"Maybe. I don't know. Anyways, all the fellas in the bar is crowdin' around the pool table, givin' advice to Sapo and shit."

120

Tombilena studied her beloved brother's face. She could discern no remorse in it.

"Go on," she said.

Campo shrugged, drank some more.

"It's about it, Tommy. Every man took his turn put a twenty in the left corner pocket by her head, that's right. She maybe was gonna split it with Gallo later. Things got hazy. Wasn't nasty or nothin', then."

"Until when?"

"Valer, he was goddam drunk, and was havin' difficulty, so he grabbed a cue and used it on her."

"You sayin' he couldn't get it up so he raped the woman with a poolstick?"

"I didn't even know what was happenin' until she was shoutin'. Valer tol' her shut up, he was usin' the thick end, and he'd paid his money, check out the pocket."

"You try to stop him?"

"Tommy, I was drunk, too. It didn't seem so bad at the time."

Tombilena stood up and showed her back to Campo. She removed the nine-millimeter Glock pistol from her purse, sucked in a large quantity of sultry air, let it out, turned around, and pointed the big ugly thing at her brother.

"Hey, Tommy! *Irmá!*" he said, smiling a little, "What's this?"

" 'And I will bring distress upon men,' " proclaimed Tombilena Gayoso, " 'because they have sinned against the Lord: and their blood shall be poured out as dust, and their flesh as the dung.' "

Before Campo could quit smiling, his sister tripped off four shots. Two of the bullets penetrated Campo's forehead a few centimeters apart above the left eye. One bullet seared his thick, curly black hair and plunged through the wood directly behind him into the living room, there ricocheting off a metal table lamp and lodging in the ceiling. The fourth shell entered Campo's open mouth and exited the rear of his skull at a forty-degree angle, gouging a deep hole in a half-rotten plank in the porch floor.

Tombilena stood still, trembling, staring at the destroyed body of her only sibling, her weapon arm at rest.

" 'Shall they not rise up suddenly that shall bite thee?' " spoke this first of Victoria China's avengers.

At that moment, Rodrigue Gayoso's Dodge Ram pickup pulled up in front of his son's house. Tombilena turned and saw her father's face behind the windshield. She lifted the gun again, propped the barrel end on her lower lip, and exhausted Rodrigue's progeny on this earth.

THE TERRIBLENESS

Dear Jesus,

The truth is there is lots left for me to learn in this life. Tombilena Gayoso who I told You about before shot and killed her brother Campo and then shot and killed herself. This was not what I had in mind when I give her the German pistol that it would end with the suicide of a good woman. Her brother deserved to die no question of it in the view of Mary Mother of God but now we have lost a valuable person. I guess the weight on Tombilena's brain of having been his judge jury and executioner kind of overwhelmed her. The mistake was to let her go alone and for this I must take the blame but if not for the horrible behavior practiced upon women by these depraved type men there would not have been this awful loss.

Jesus I am getting at something and that is my fear being no matter what we of Mary Mother of God do the terribleness goes on and on. I and the others who take as our guide Your Word and the teachings of Hilda Brausen stand determined to combat the increasing terror. I believe personally there are evils on the horizon beyond anything any person of this earth has thought of. As Isaiah warned do I instruct my sisters I say to them that are of a fearful heart be strong fear not behold your God will come with vengeance but Jesus is vengeance enough?

Your faithful
Marble

SOUTHERN COMFORT

*R*ODRIGUE GAYOSO was slumped buzzard-still on his bar-stool until Wesson Lesson bumped into him, knocking an empty shot glass from the practically catatonic fisherman's fist.

"Sorry, man," said the perpetrator, reaching for Rodrigue and holding on to the seated patron's left shoulder, steadying himself. "I'm a right clumsy sonofabuck, 'specially when I'm drunk. Get you another'n. What you drinkin'?"

Rodrigue Gayoso, devastated by the loss of both his son and daughter, had been poisoning himself at a steady clip for four hours in the Saturn Bar on St. Claude Avenue in New Orleans. During the three days immediately following the hideous double deaths, Rodrigue had become numb. He'd handled the funeral arrangements, witnessed the entombment of his children, and not taken a drink until this afternoon, driving into the city to do it, not wanting to remain any longer in the vicinity of the greatest tragedy of his life.

"Say, pardner, you breathin'?" Wes asked. "Name your brand."

The bartender, a short, stubby, mostly bald middle-aged man with a weak-lidded left eye named Bosco Brouillard, set a fresh shot on the bar in front of Rodrigue and said to Wes, "Early Times."

Wes pulled a couple of crumpled dollar bills from his left front pants pocket and tossed them toward Bosco.

"On me," he said. "If this fella's dead, I'll drink it."

"My children," said Rodrigue, moving only his lips. "My children are dead."

Wes Lesson was in his late thirties, a fair-haired, medium-sized man nursing a slight paunch. He toppled westward and landed on the stool next to the morose Isleño.

"Say what? Your kids is dead?"

Rodrigue nodded. "My wife, Feroza, she rest in peace. My children, Campo, Tombilena, now also."

The weather-wrinkled and sun-blackened fifty-two-year-old crabber committed a half turn, lifted the newly poured liquor, and drained the container with a sudden jerk. He rolled the glass with his flat, heavily calloused fingers, then replaced it gently on the mahogany countertop.

"Boy, that's rough," Wes Lesson said. "I got me a strange but beautiful daughter named Marble I'd hate to lose. There's not much a parent can do once they're big enough to turn a doorknob. Then on, either they're hunters or the hunted, ain't they?"

Rodrigue Gayoso grunted. He opened and raised his crimson eyes just enough to verify the person to whom he was speaking.

"My name's Lesson, Wes Lesson. Let me buy you another."

"*Obrigado.* I am Rodrigue Gayoso."

Wes signaled to Bosco Brouillard for two more drinks, and the bartender brought them.

"You from Delacroix?" Bosco asked. "Heard on the news about a double murder out there the other day."

"Yes. Those were my children."

"Well, I am sorry as hell for you, Mr. Gayoso," said Wes. "The world is gotten about as wicked as it can get, I guess."

"*Foi um ato muito bruto. Custa-me trabalho crêo-lo.*"

"Can't say I disagree, sir. Whatever it is you said."

Wes swallowed half of his Crown Royal and water, shook his head, and said, " 'And the Lord said unto Satan, From whence comest thou?' "

" 'From goin' to and fro in the earth,' " answered Bosco, " 'and from walkin' up and down in it.' "

"What can you do?" Wes said.

"*Lamentar,*" said Rodrigue.

"What?" asked Wes.

"To mourn," Bosco said. "The lot of the living is to mourn."

"Jesus," said Wes.

Bosco smiled and winked his weak-lidded left eye.

"Exactly," he said.

$\mathcal{T}$HE $\mathcal{G}$IFT

ON MARBLE LESSON'S SEVENTEENTH BIRTHDAY, at a party thrown for her at Mary Mother of God, she made an announcement that both surprised and delighted her fellow crusaders. An ovarian egg extracted from Helga Grandeza had been inseminated *in vitro* with the sperm of an anonymous donor, and the fertilized egg was then inserted into Marble's womb. Marble was impregnated with Helga's child, which the younger woman would bear on behalf of the collective. Amniocentesis could not be performed until the fourteenth week of pregnancy, Marble informed her cohorts, but if the child were female—which they were convinced it would be—she and Helga had decided to name her Hilda Brausen Grandeza-Lesson. This news was greeted by astonished gasps, followed by applause and an onslaught of feverish embracing.

128

"This is a gift to all of us," said Marble. "A present to the women of the world. Hilda will be able to carry our message to the threshold of the twenty-second century."

Following the festivities at the center, Marble went home and found her father and a companion sitting in the front room of the house she shared with him on Upper Line, drinking whiskey. Both men were in an advanced state of inebriation.

"H'lo, sweetheart. Happy Birthday," Wes Lesson said. "Meet my frien', Rodrigue. Rodrigue, this's my daughter, Marble. My one and only strange and beautiful daughter. Rodrigue's a fisherman from Delacroix. Both his kids died recently. It's a awful story, honey. Worst story I ever heard."

Marble walked over to where the last of the Gayosos sat half-conscious in a moth-eaten, rotting brown armchair, his eyes seven-eighths closed. She stood next to the chair and gazed down at Rodrigue. A large silver cross attached to a thin neck chain rested on his chest, the sculpted Christ figure rising and falling with each breath.

" 'For I reckon,' " said Marble, " 'that the sufferings of this present time are not worthy to be compared with the glory that shall be revealed in us.' "

"That's right, sweetheart," Wes Lesson said. "You tell it."

Marble looked at her drunken hulk of a father, and her eyes filled with tears.

" 'Arise, Daddy,' " she said, " 'and walk through the land in the length of it and in the breadth of it; for I will give it unto thee.' "

Wesson Lesson raised his head and smiled at his daughter.

"Baby," he said, "I know goddam well you would. It's just that I ain't really up to it."

ℸHE 𝓛AST
OF THE 𝒥UST

RAID ON CHARM SCHOOL
EXPOSES FEMALE
VIGILANTE SOCIETY

NEW ORLEANS, Aug. 28 (SNS)—New Orleans police, assisted by criminal enforcement agents of the U.S. Bureau of Alcohol, Tobacco and Firearms, staged a late-night raid on the Hilda Brausen Charm School on Venus Street in the Gentilly Terrace section of this city.

A spokesperson for the BATF revealed that the modeling and manners academy, patronized by many of the city's most prominent families, was operating a clandestine escort service, dozens of whose male clients were murdered by women from whom they had expected sexual favors in exchange for the escort fee.

Arrested in the raid were fifteen women, including four

minors. The school's owner-operator, Hilda Brausen Grandeza-Lesson, eluded capture and is believed to be in hiding somewhere in the New Orleans area.

Seized at the scene were numerous automatic and semiautomatic weapons, an assortment of crossbows, swordcanes, switchblade knives, and handguns, along with a large quantity of China White heroin that government agents estimate would carry a street value of over two million dollars.

According to federal agent Lance Boyle, Jr., who has been investigating the radical feminist underground movement of recent years, a vigilante group known as "Die Brausenkriegers" (the Brausen Warriors), whose philosophy is based on the writings and legend of the German feminist thinker Hilda Brausen, are, Boyle says, "dedicated to cleansing the earth of dominant males. Their purpose is to reduce the role of men to that of drones in a beehive. The Brausens believe the sole purpose of the male is to service the queen."

Hilda Brausen died under mysterious circumstances during World War I, apparently while masquerading as a man in the German army. Her namesake, Hilda Brausen Grandeza-Lesson, who is believed to be in her mid-thirties, is the daughter of Sister Marble Lesson, founder of the Mary Mother of God Rescue Crusade, an international organization devoted to the welfare of women worldwide.

Sister Lesson, who had been recognized by many humanitarian organizations and world governments for her selfless works, and who was often spoken of during her lifetime as a potential recipient of the Nobel Prize, was beheaded ten years ago by rebel tribesmen on the outskirts of Kismayu, Somalia. Sister Lesson had gone to Somalia to participate as a member of the planning commission of the Mary Mother of God Pan-African Condom Manufacturing Co.

$\mathcal{N}$IGHT $\mathcal{L}$ETTER

Dear Jesus,

Ever since the death of my mother I have lived in fear of this moment the time that I would be confronted with a major decision and have no one special person to whom I could turn for advice. This is why I have chosen to write to You knowing that my mother was Your faithful correspondent from her childhood until her demise in the jungle.

I am writing this at midnight in the attic room of a house on Ptolemy Street in Algiers Louisiana where I am a fugitive and will have to leave tomorrow night. The question I am asking myself is how best to continue the struggle. Unlike my mother I have not been a religious person and do not consider myself a Christian so it is certainly strange for me to be writing a letter to Jesus I know. It is just that I am cornered and need a direction to go. I remember as a child my mother telling me that You were the only man who had ever lived who had not in life or even death disappointed a woman. She used to sing to me the hymn What A Friend I Have in Jesus over and over at my bedtime. I miss her more and more Jesus all the time. Marble Lesson was a saint if there ever could be one I am sure you agree.

I know a woman named Viridiana Temoign Crosby who has a church called the New Idea of the Fresh Start in a little town in Arkansas called Daytime that is where I plan to go from here. It is not exactly a place on the beaten path and Virdy believes I will find a safe haven there at least for a while. If You have an answer for me Jesus You know how to find me. If You are in touch with my mother please tell her I love and miss her and that I am doing my best to carry on the work back here on what she used to call the Big Angry Planet.

Sincerely yours
Hilda Brausen Grandeza-Lesson

$\mathcal{A}$ $\mathcal{N}$OSE
FOR A $\mathcal{N}$OSE

"$\mathcal{I}$T'S NOT THAT I DISAGREE with you, H.B., but there's got to be a purpose the Lord made men, other than just for matin' purposes, that is."

"Virdy, my feelin' is the Lord, providin' there is one and that He had anythin' to do with it, did women an injustice when He failed to equip 'em with the capacity for self-reproduction. There're other species capable of it. Why not us?"

Viridiana Temoign Crosby, pastor of the Church of the New Idea of the Fresh Start, and Hilda Brausen Grandeza-Lesson, a fugitive from justice, wanted in the state of Louisiana for murder and drug trafficking, were walking in the birch woods behind the New Idea building in Daytime, Arkansas. The late-October weather was unusually warm, and the women were comfortable in midmorning without coats. Hilda had found refuge in Daytime, at least temporarily; Sister Crosby always had been sympathetic to H.B.'s radical feminist activities. In addition, Hilda's famous mother, the late Marble Lesson, was a legend among progressive feminist thinkers the world over, a fact that lent her daughter considerable credence.

"It was the noses really gave 'em the red ass," said Hilda. "The press just went nuts about it."

"Noses?"

"Yeah. Back in the early days of Mary Mother of God, when my mama was with the organization, they had a secret core group called Die Brausenkriegers would avenge particularly nasty abuses."

"I seem to remember hearin' somethin' about this from my aunt Mamie Eisenhower Temoign. Wasn't there some kinda deal they were supposed to've murdered a bunch of fishermen raped a woman?"

"Right. Victoria China Realito was her name. She insisted that Die Brausenkriegers bring her the noses of the men who'd assaulted her, as proof of their execution and to send a message to men everywhere."

"Why noses?"

"When the Japanese invaded Korea in 1597, they lopped off the noses of over twenty thousand Koreans as proof of kills. The soldiers brought the evidence back to Japan and buried 'em in what was called the Thousand-Nose Tomb. Apparently, Victoria Realito had read about this and started the nose-takin' trend. We revived the tradition durin' our extracurricular activities at the Hilda Brausen Charm School in New Orleans."

"What'd y'all do with the noses?"

"If the men were married, we mailed 'em to their wives. Otherwise, we tossed 'em into the compost heap for our organic vegetable garden. Virdy, we grew the best squash and tomatoes you ever could expect to eat. There's no doubt in my mind it's the unrestricted use of pesticides has caused serious brain damage to countless Americans. You know, if a person really thinks about it, there's so much wrong with the world already, and more goin' haywire all the time, could be it won't never be possible to fix."

CODA

THE PASSION OF
HYPOLITE CORTEZ

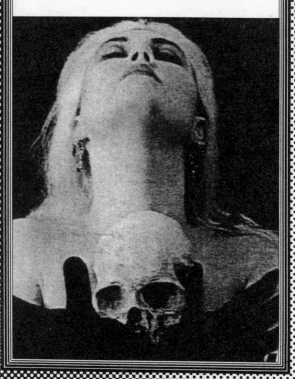

✝HE ℙASSION

ℙARSHAL LEE cracked open the monkey's skull with a ball peen hammer, picked it up, and drank the fluid from the deceased simian's hypothalamus gland. He was a determined individual. If this was what it took to regain the exclusive affections of Hypolite Cortez, damn straight he'd do it. It and anything else that seemed logical to Miss Consuelo Yesso, Parshal's advisor in matters involving love and finance.

Parshal Lee was an artist, a portrait painter who set up shop daily next to the north fence of Jackson Square in New Orleans. He was thirty-eight years old, a native of Meridian, Mississippi, a place to which he had no desire to return. Parshal had not been in Meridian since his mother, Zolia Versalles Lee, was buried four years before across the street from the Dixie Boys Field. He had no living relatives that he knew of other than an eighty-four-year-old bastard uncle named Get-Down Lucky, who was part Gypsy and sold Bibles door-to-door in Dothan, Alabama. It was this uncle who had informed Parshal at Zolia Lee's funeral that the meaning of life was based on a simple concept. "It ain't what you eat," said Get-Down Lucky, "it's the way how you chew it."

Parshal's father, Roy L Lee, had disappeared the day before his son's fourteenth birthday. Roy L—he had no middle name, only an initial he'd taken himself so that he would have something to write in on forms that requested one—was believed to have fled Meridian in order to avoid prosecution for grave robbing. He and a one-armed Salvadoran refugee named Arturo Trope, who had worked as an undertaker's assistant in a Meridian funeral parlor, had been apprehended exhuming newly buried bodies in order to steal rings, necklaces, and other valuable items decorating the corpses. Both men had skipped town on bail, and two months later Arturo Trope had been shot to death during the commission of an armed robbery of a jewelry store on Capitol Street in Jackson. Roy L had not been seen or heard from since the cemetery scam. Parshal considered his daddy dead and himself a free agent. All he had to make his way in the world was his God-given artistic talent. Roy L, Parshal figured, had nothing to do with that.

Parshal sat on the porch of his rented bungalow on Spain Street in the Marigny, chasing the bitter taste of monkey gland fluid with Rebel Yell. His brain was obsessed by thoughts of his erstwhile girlfriend, Hypolite Cortez, and the fact that she had abandoned him in favor of a woman. Hypolite now lived with an exotic dancer named Irma Soon, a Panamanian-Chinese who simulated copulation with a rock python six nights a week at Big Nig's Gauchos 'n' Gals Club on Pelican Avenue in Algiers. Parshal was hoping that Miss Yesso's prescription would inspire Hypolite to return to her senses and to him. She had given no reason for her defection, merely left a note on her red sateen pillow embroidered in yellow with intertwined initials *P* and *H*, that said: "Parshal you took care of me best you could but I have fallen for Irma Soon who I believe is my destiny. Our two years together have been good however love is got to be better than good and only with Irma Soon have I felt what is commonly called ecstasy. I hope one day you will know for yourself with someone the way I feel with Irma. Luv to you and I mean it, Hypolite."

Parshal Lee had given Hypolite's note to Consuelo Yesso, who rolled the paper into a tiny ball, dipped it into a powder made of flywings and lizard tongues, and told Parshal to swallow it, which he had. By ingesting Hypolite's note, garnished with these purposeful ingredients, Miss Yesso explained, Parshal would cause his beloved to dream of him and force Hypolite to reconsider her situation. Miss Yesso had handed him the monkey's skull wrapped with aluminum foil and promised to continue her efforts toward accomplishing Hypolite and Parshal's reconciliation. Parshal paid the *bruja* what she asked, and tried to put a hopeful spin on his thoughts, but he knew that it would take more than Miss Yesso's powers to bring back Hypolite Cortez.

"Hey, Parshal! Parshal Lee!"

Parshal broke out of his trance and saw Avenue Al, a neighbor, standing on the sidewalk. Al was wearing a dyed-purple mohair suit, which he called his "goat coat," and was propped up on crutches, necessitated by his having taken a hard fall and broken both knees while leaving Teresa's Tite Spot Lounge in the Bywater two months before. Avenue Al, a sixty-year-old former professional wrestler whose claim to fame was that he had bitten off one of Dick the Bruiser's earlobes, was suing Teresa for damages. His plan, he told everyone, was to take the money and retire in Cebu City, the Philippines, where he had once wrestled an ape. "Fell in love a dozen times in six days," he claimed, "and never even got the clap."

"Come on, Parshal," Avenue Al shouted, "let's go! Trumpet Shorty havin' a funeral for his pit bull, Louis Armstrong, jus' passed. Be the firs' dog have a second-line since dat rabid Airedale, Dagoo, hads to be put down in '71."

*G*REAT *E*XPECTATIONS

"*N*OBODY CARES *what* you do in New Orleans, but everyone wants to know what it is."

"I like for folks to know what I'm up to, so they know what to *expec'*."

Parshal Lee sat at the bar in Teresa's Tite Spot, nursing a Bombay on the rocks, half-listening to Beverly Waverly and Caspiana Pleasant, two café-au-lait transvestites, converse. Mostly, he contemplated his unhappy circumstance.

"Parshal. Parshal, baby," said Caspiana. "Why you so morose?"

"What's morose?" asked Beverly.

"Unnormally quiet and broodish," Caspiana answered. "What's up, Parshal? You might can tell us girls."

"Hypolite left me."

"Aw, honey," said Beverly, putting a meaty, hairy forearm

around Parshal's neck, "ain't that a bitch. Some women just don't got good sense. No man she could get better'n you."

"Didn't leave me for a man. Took up with an exotic dancer over in Algiers. Woman name Irma Soon."

Caspiana gasped. "You mean the China girl porks her own-self with a snake? Used to she work at Tickfaw Fouquet's Crawl Inn?"

"Half Chinese. Half from Panama."

"Shit, baby," said Caspiana, "that's rough. You need it, me an' Beverly, we zoom ya."

"Ain' be pussy, 'xactly," said Beverly, "but it defi'tely da nex' bes' thing."

" 'Preciate your concern, ladies, but I'm workin' on this in my own way."

"Okay, baby," said Caspiano, "but we here for ya."

"I hoid such a terr'ble thing, today," Beverly said. "Was on the TV news."

"What dat?"

"Russian man was sentence to death for killlin' more'n fifty people. Men, boys, women, an' girls. Ate parts their bodies, mostly tips of their tongues and genitalia."

"Saint Rose of Lima!" cried Caspiana, crossing herself.

"Man was fifty-six years old, and impotent. Only way he could complete a sexual act was by torturin' an' killin' someone. Russian papers called him the 'Forest Strip Killer,' after the place where he dump mos' the bodies."

"Lord have mercy. He jus' cut folks apart, huh?"

"What da news say."

"An' some people thinkin' *we* weird!"

"If everyone was so well adjusted as you two," said Parshal, "wouldn't never be no more wars."

Caspiana smiled, leaned over, and kissed him on the left cheek.

"Bless you, baby," she said. "But you jus' seen us on our best behavior. We might can be some tacky bitches sometime."

"You want Hypolite back," said Beverly, "best you stay in her face. Let her know you there for her."

Caspiana shook her curly gold wig. "Don't believe it, sugar. Liable push the lady further away. Besides, she an' this snake charmer in the first flush of their love. No way to buck that. My advice, darlin', wait it out. You a good *man*, after all. Hypolite come back aroun'. She don't, somethin' turn up."

Parshal finished off his Bombay, thanked Caspiana and Beverly for their commiseration, and walked outside. It was a hot night; the air was even heavier than ordinary in July. He went to his car, a two-year-old blue Thunderbird, unlocked the driver's side door, and was about to get in, thinking to cruise over to Algiers, check out his rival Irma Soon's terpsichorean snake act, when Parshal felt a cold, hard object enter the outer part of his left ear.

"Y'all don' min'," a high-pitched voice said, "my name is Carjack Jack an' I gon' be y'all's designated driver tonight."

Out of the corner of his left eye, Parshal saw a skinny, balding white man in his mid-thirties, wearing a blue Hawaiian shirt decorated with yellow parrots and red flowers. A bright purple scar the width of a trouser zipper ran down the center of his nose from bridge to tip. Parshal started to turn toward him but as he did the man inserted the gun barrel deeper into Parshal's ear, forcing his head away, then removed the weapon briefly before bringing the butt down hard on the soft spot at the back of Parshal's head. Parshal collapsed against the car and the man opened the door, shoved Parshal's limp shape into the backseat, took the keys from the door lock, climbed behind the steering wheel, and closed himself inside. He cranked the engine and grinned, exposing a row of rotten teeth.

"Hellfire!" Carjack Jack screeched, shifting the T-Bird into gear and tearing away from the curb. "We got us some *miles* to go before we sleep. *Miles*. Course, y'all're already sleepin', ain't ya? Well, as them pussies out in California say, this here's the first day of the rest of our lives, an' a life is a terrible thing to waste. Or is that a mind is bad to waste? Hell, *I* don't mind! Waste not, want not. Two peas in a pod. Damn the *Defiant!* Ain't *no* business like *show* business. Fasten your seatbelt, buddy, this gon' be a *bumpy* fuckin' ride."

THE BIG BITE

HYPOLITE CORTEZ sat at a ringside table in Big Nig's Gauchos 'n' Gals Club, sipping sparkling water through a straw. She was twenty-two years old, a smidge more than five foot two, had never weighed a hundred pounds in her life, had huge black eyes, severely arched Chinese eyebrows, and permitted her midnight black hair to fall slightly below her seventeen-inch waist. Above the nipple of her left breast was a three-quarter-inch in circumference dark blue, star-shaped mole that Hypolite referred to as "where the Arab bit me." This mole Hypolite had inherited from her maternal grandmother, Ephémère Plaire, who told Hypolite that her own paternal grandmother, Pilar LaLa, had borne this identical mark. The first time Irma Soon saw it, she experienced a spontaneous orgasm.

The lights dimmed, a drum rolled, and from offstage a husky female voice, that of Bruma "Big Nig" Goma, the proprietress herself, announced: "Get ready, Eddie! Chase dat frown, Miz Brown! You ain't seen poon 'til you see Miz Soon! Here she be, di-rek from Mandinga, Panama, da soipent princess, doin' an exclusive performance of 'La Gran Mordedura'—a specialmost dance she create herself that been banned in most parts da Orient—Miz . . . Oima . . . Sooooonnn!"

The lavender curtains parted, revealing a diminutive woman whose body was crisscrossed with several rivet-studded black leather belts. Miss Soon's most intimate part was fully exposed, however, while stretched across her tiny breasts and relaxed around her neck was a reticulated creature the color of Delaware River mud. The patrons of the half-filled Gauchos 'n' Gals Club howled and applauded at this sight. A slow version of "Little Egypt" emanated from the band pit, prompting the lithe Filipina to begin her routine, which consisted mostly of waving arms and undulating hips. This tepid dance continued for several minutes, during which time the reptile remained composed, placid, unstirred; until Irma Soon gently but firmly grasped its head with her right hand and placed it directly between her legs.

At this point the patrons, some of whom gasped audibly, froze in their seats. The dancer closed her eyes, thrust her pelvis forward, and bent backward incrementally, slowly, tortuously, or so it seemed to those in rapt attention, until her head touched the floor. To all appearances, the python's head had disappeared inside Irma Soon. Hypolite Cortez shivered as she watched her lover manipulate the reptile. As easily as Miss Soon had accommodated it, she withdrew the lubricated cranium and with an agonizing absence of haste, sinuously resumed an upright position. Holding the python by her right hand just behind the head, Irma positioned it face-to-face and flicked her own pointy tongue toward it. The music reached a crescendo and Irma twirled with the snake, the two creatures' tongues darting at one another until the dancer whirled them offstage.

The audience whistled and clapped their hands, hardly believing what they had just witnessed. Hypolite smiled demurely and sat still, proud and deeply in love, thoroughly enchanted.

"Dass it, gauchos 'n' gals," boomed Bruma Goma. "Ain't another performer like Irma Soon this side o' Subic Bay! Let her know y'all appreciate her art! Open up fo' dis Filipina baby!"

The patrons continued to shout, whistle, and applaud until the curtains closed. It was not Irma Soon's habit to take a parting bow. She had explained to Hypolite that once the connection with her audience had been made, she preferred to leave it unblemished, having no desire to break the spell or alter the feeling she had engendered. To her fans, Irma remained forever in character.

The band segued into a waltz-like treatment of "The Fat Man" and several couples, some of the same or similar sex, rose to dance. Hypolite dipped a hand between her gooey thighs and closed her eyes as she massaged herself, holding in her mind the impossibly beautiful image of Irma Soon and the python locked in their forbidden embrace.

TWO FOR THE ROAD

"*Y*OU gonna harm me?"

Carjack Jack looked back over his right shoulder at Parshal, wrinkled his lips toward his zipper-nose, and laughed.

"Hell, pardner," he said, returning his eyes to the road, "I ain't no demon. Don't do no brutalizin' 'less it's essential. Sorry I had to sock you back there, but a man has to know what he has to do when it has to be done. Mack Daddy of all Mack Daddies told me that ten years ago. City jail, Montgomery, Alabama. Copperhead Kane was his name. Famous man, famous. Had him a escort network from Alabama to Illinois. Copperhead Kane, yeah. The man in*vented* phone sex. That's a fact."

Parshal lay on the backseat, still woozy from the blow to

his head. He noticed that neither his hands nor his feet had been bound. Carjack Jack sped the blue Bird along Chef Menteur Highway.

"What're you gonna do with me, then?" Parshal asked him.

"Ain't quite decided. You want me to drop you someplace in particular? I'm thinkin' on headin' up north, myself. What's your name, anyway?"

"Lee. Parshal Lee."

"Just call me C.J. Best you don't know my family name."

Parshal thought about Hypolite Cortez. He wondered whether the years she had worked as a teenage prostitute for the Hilda Brausen Charm School had unduly influenced her gender preference. He had to admit that despite his unselfish efforts of a sexual nature, Hypolite had never really responded to him as did other women. Something had been missing in their relationship. Parshal watched the blackness pass for a minute before he spoke.

"You don't mind, C.J., maybe I'll just tag along with you. Need to put some space between me and a kind of unhealthy situation here, anyway."

"Guess I could do with some comp'ny, Parshal. Ten to one it's a renegade female messed up your mind."

"How'd you guess?"

C.J. laughed. "It's a epidemic. Happenin' all over the so-called civilized world. Copperhead Kane predicted it back when. The people ain't starvin' for food are starvin' for answers. Things is got too complicated for words, or ain't you been payin' attention?"

"Not close enough, I guess."

"Take this show I seen on TV one night in the joint, called *Down to Earth*. You ever watched it?"

"No," said Parshal. "What is it?"

"See, these couples go out on a date for the first time, and one of 'em thinks it's the greatest thing. Usually they had sex of some type on the date. So they bring on the one of 'em thinks the date was great, all that. Then the other one comes on and totally tears up the date, hated it, had bad sex, bad breath, bad manners, the guy's hairpiece fell off while he was performin' cunnilingus on her. They'll say anything."

"Prob'ly it's in the script. They just sayin' what was wrote for 'em to say and ain't none of it happened."

"Wrong, Mr. Lee. Nobody could make up this stuff. This guy had eyebrows took up half his face won with the best story."

"Wha'd he tell?"

"You won't believe it. Said he and this girl go out to a nice dinner. She has the lamb chops, eats the parsley, so he figures she's both classy and healthy, yeah?"

"Oh?"

"Yeah. So, they go to a movie."

"What movie?"

"A Spanish picture, somethin' European, where all the women got long noses and by the end the men are wearin' spike heels and lipstick and complainin' how they don't get enough sex."

"Ho!"

"They go next to the girl's apartment, where the guy says she's all over him like an electric blanket. Get this, the guy actually says this: 'I got my eel out and she's doin' the popsicle!' That's what he says! The audience is dyin'!"

"He got his eel out."

"His eel, yeah. Then it comes."

"His eel?"

"No, no. The good part of his story."

"The good part."

"He grabs her crotch, and guess what?"

"She's a guy, too."

"Right! Right! Of course, she's really a guy!"

"Is the guy who was supposed to be a girl on the show?"

"Yeah, yeah. And guess what? He comes on after Eyebrows gives his version and denies everything! You believe that, Mr. Lee? Completely and entirely says Eyebrows is out of his goddam mind!"

"Jesus."

"Now, here's the killer."

"Don't tell me."

"Shit, Parshal, can you guess? Can you?"

"She offers to prove she's a woman."

"Correct! Yeah, yeah! Right on the air! She pulls up her skirt an' shows her pelt! The audience is goin' batshit. The host is lyin' on the couch, chokin' to death. This Nancy starts paradin' up an' down the stage, like on a runway, got his jewels tucked up so nothin' shows. Man, you never, *never* seen nothin' like this."

"What's Eyebrows doin'?"

"Okay, get this: Eyebrows attacks Nancy."

"Eyebrows *attacks* Nancy?!"

"Tries to get at his dick."

"Holy shit."

"Nancy karate chops him in the back of the neck, and Eyebrows goes down hard on his nose, which bleeds."

"Holy shit."

"The security guys come out an' separate the two. Nancy is outtahermind handsdown havin' the greatest time of her life! She's smilin', throwin' kisses to the audience."

"You have to admit, C.J., it's a special place would allow a program like that on the air."

Carjack Jack nodded his red crew-cut head several times and laughed.

"Mr. Lee," he said, "I got no doubt in my mind but that there ain't never been and won't never will be another country like this one in the history of planet earth."